THE INNKEEPER'S DIARY

MICHAEL KENT

THE INNKEEPER'S DIARY

Copyright © 2022 Michael Kent

All rights reserved.

ISBN: **9798700973908**

0

This book is dedicated to my grandchildren,

Apollo, Holland, and Orion,

As well as that little child in every one of us,

That still dares to dream, to imagine, and to wonder.

FORWORD

"You should write a book", they said....

Hurricane Michael was a pivotal, life changing event for many, each of us learning to cope with our situations in different ways. I found that posting and sharing commentary on social media was an unexpected, yet welcomed avenue in which to express myself, as I went on my journey to make sense of it all.

There were obstacles disguised as fear, doubt, and uncertainty, as if anyone could possibly be interested in what I had to say. I began to post my commentary on social media in order to gain feedback, if any.

It was there that I realized the true power of a kind word, or just a short note from someone who took the time to let me know that it was appreciated, and that I should keep writing. It was the fuel I needed to stay at it, and I appreciate your comments beyond words.

A few days after Hurricane Michael made landfall, my son advised me to write down everything that was happening throughout my ordeal. Pages of random notes turned into short narratives, and I began to get more creative with the journal entries. It was through these notations that I discovered an unknown talent for writing. I found it therapeutic for me, and it helped me cope with the unfortunate turn of events that had recently encompassed my life.

My comments posted on social media were met with such positive responses, that I continued my jottings to the point where it appeared to some that a book could be in the making. The diary entries evolved from reflections of life before the storm, to observations about the present, and then into a realm of fictional stories, all relating in varying degrees to life at a small inn on the beach, a category five hurricane, and how I found a way to deal with a devastating loss, while finding myself again and rising up and out of the rubble. (There are also a few talking animals here and there.)

After I felt that the manuscript was finished, I entered into the world of formatting, spell-checking, and editing, which was each a project within itself, and I had quite an adventure designing and producing the book's cover.

I would like to thank everyone that has taken an interest in my writings and ramblings, the support you have offered me has been monumental in my pursuit of actually publishing this memoir. Without your comments, my thoughts may have merely drifted away.

I took a notion to document the narratives and stories in the form of a diary, and in one of my scribbling's, I imagined placing the diary into a bottle, then casting it into the sea.

So, there I went, walking down to the beach at dusk;
Bottle and camera in hand……

TABLE OF CONTENTS

Introduction	09
Finding the Vista	11
Another day in Paradise	13
First Report	17
Dad, You Need to Write	19
Ground Zero	21
The 12 Days of Michael	23
Evacuation Post	25
Rearview Mirror	27
Natures Refugees	29
Scenic Route	31
Saint Joseph's Sea Dragon	32
Beach-Henge	33
The New Normal	35
His Name Was Howard	37
Buena Vista Information and Policies	39
After the Tempest	41
Castles in the Sand	43

	6
Spaceship Earth	45
The Ninja Chronicle	47
The Smallest Percentage	51
He's Not My Dog	55
The Reef	59
Angels among Us	79
The Vacation Mindset	81
Anniversarial Retrospect	83
Omega Man	87
The Versatility of Viewpoint	91
The Forgotten Forest: Captain's Chronicles	93
Photo Shoot	95
Forgotten Forest: The Story of the Gulf Foods Bear	99
Day of the Pelican	111
The Miracle	117
Autobiography: September 17, 1961	119
Autobiography: The Japan Diaries	125
Autobiography: Going Home	135
Life of Coonie	137
The Shepherd of the Seas	142
The Eagle's Opus	143

The Imminent Predators	147
Paranormal Activities	153
The Ghost of the Buena Vista	155
Quarantined: Day 15	161
Quarantined: Day 23	165
A Pleasant Distraction	169
The Messenger	171
Treasure	173
Dad and Jesus	177
Category Eight; a Fictional Premise	181
Beautiful World	189
Captain Davey	191
The Phantom of the Aqua	207
Back to School	213
In the Realm of the Heavens	215
An Unlikely Minimalist	217
Acknowledgments	223
About the Author	225

INTRODUCTION

Upon notice by a few select individuals of the proprietary nature, there came to pass an interest in an area along the shore, for the purpose of settlement, adjacent to the harboring comforts of Saint Joseph's Port. This village began modestly, offering a retreat for even the weariest of worriers; a soon to be haven for sea fishers, sun seekers, and escape artists, lending itself to the propensity of the locals to frequent the taverns, while engaging in the imbibery and debauchery that resided therein.

And as it were, the days of life in the little hamlet by the sea became perpetual as the tides. The timely regimen of the waves, the daily repetition of sunrises and sunsets, and the temperatures of the seasons had manifested quite a bustling of local residents, or "natives" as they might boast, over a pint or two. The wealthy gypsies would construct encampments along the shore, and then gather together, establishing "councils" and "departments", in order to subject themselves to self-discipline, while ensuring that others do the same.

I professed to be none other than a modest innkeeper, a wearied soldier of fortune harboring the remains of a misspent youth, seeking peace and solitude during my remaining days on this earth; and as the circumstances were so, that I might remain host at such inn, for a period that offered time to write essays and reflections in a diary, and to keep one as such for reference to others.

Whilst upon this notion, the little hamlet by the sea experienced a tempest of a lifetime's proportion; a violent storm to surpass all others; forever changing the lives of all that lay in its path…

10

FINDING THE VISTA

February, 2003

It had been over thirty years since the tornado took the house on the hill. Life had been a long series of events, as life generally goes. I had my share of ups and downs, successes and failures, moments of uncertainty as well as confidence. I saw new life in the births of children, and said goodbye to loved ones passing from this world. I witnessed the horrors of addictions, alcoholism, and the suffering they caused. At one time or another, I experienced anguish, joy, depression, happiness, sadness, and all emotions in between.

Along the way, I was seeking, as we all do, my own place of peace in this world, my own solace, my own home. One day in my travels, I came upon a small six room inn on a beach that had a for sale sign in the window. It was somewhat downtrodden, with a red dirt parking lot. I was intrigued, and pulled over to look around. One of the doors were open, so I glanced inside. The furniture was dated, and there was a piece of wall art in a frame that must have fallen to the floor, breaking the glass, yet someone apparently secured it back to the wall with large pieces of duct tape. The faucet was steadily dripping and there was no one around. I walked around the little motel to the back that faced the beach, and turned the corner.

It was then that I saw the most amazing sight: A panoramic view of a beautiful beach; an estuary where the earth met the ocean in subtle transition, the coastline extending in a curvature from as far as I could see to the left, then to as far as I could see to the right. I witnessed the rage of the ocean, and the calm of the clouds above. The breeze tickled the sea oats, as a host of pelicans floated by on gentle currents of air, their wings outstretched in total freedom. In the center of the scene lay the path of the sun, and as it set, I saw Gods hand paint the sky in brilliant colors from a seemingly infinite cosmic palette…

As the sun disappeared from my sight, the stars began to reveal themselves, and I could then see beyond the blue barrier of daylight, and look into the far reaches of the universe above.

This was it.
This place was my peace.
This place was to be my solace.
This was to be my home.

It took many years to achieve the goal, but I remained focused on my pursuit, until one day I found a way to purchase the little motel on the beach. The debt burden was high, consuming the income beyond its limits, requiring full attention on my behalf to make it work, but it mattered not to me. There were moments of exhaustion, frustration, and doubt, but all I had to do was walk out on the back deck, pause for a moment, and witness the spectacle of his creation. It was all worth it.

It was there that I felt closest to God.

ANOTHER DAY IN PARADISE

The ocean. Just the word sounds immense; and justifiably so, the oceans cover more of the Earth's surface than all its land masses combined. Its majesty intrigues us and its allure beckons us, drawing us to it like a magnet to steel.

Whether it be the peace and serenity, the sun and water, or perhaps our subliminal need to return to the seas, where life began; people would always flock to the little beach, some driving far distances, even if only for a day or two. We would host guests from as far away as England, Germany and Sweden, or as close in as Alabama, Georgia, and Tennessee.

Many would return, and became regular guests to the point that rarely did I have a guest that had not been there before. Most felt like family, and they felt at home when they were there. It was not uncommon for reservations to be made with a first name only, or for returning guests to arrive while I was cleaning rooms, only to jump in and offer a helping hand. Often, I would see guests arriving as total strangers become friends over the course of their stay, and when departing, sharing phone numbers, taking photos, and hugging each other like family, while planning their next visit.

On any given day, we might witness dolphins cresting the surface of the water, or pelicans in formations of flight gliding across the horizon. Perhaps seagulls flocking overhead, soon to be lured in by a guest with a French fry or cracker, while little white sand crabs scurried among the dunes. Often referred to as ghost crabs, they would move "sideways", with their eyes focused on you, their foreboding claw constantly drawn and at the ready, as to portray a strong statement of defense. The little residents among the sea oats were always prepared to retreat into their burrows under the sand at the first sign of impending danger. On one occasion, we were host to a sea turtle nest next to the staircase that led down to the water's edge. What a joyous occasion it was to witness them hatch, and follow their journey toward the moonlight and into the sea.

Life around the little motel became routine in a way, there were usually one or more guests checking in, and others checking out.

The building was so old that maintenance became a daily duty, and I kept a perpetual list of repairs to be done. One afternoon my friend Dave and I were building deck chairs, when a guest approached us.

"Did you hear about the hurricane forming South of Cuba?" He asked. "They say it might be a strong one, like a category 2."

I did not think much of it, as I had seen my share of tropical storms and hurricanes come and go over the years, to the point of becoming complacent about the topic. By that evening, the storm had strengthened, and the projections pointed it heading somewhere between Panama City and Apalachicola, Florida. "Well, isn't that something", I thought. "I happen to live right in between the two." I walked over to the grocery store, where the cashiers and a few locals were watching the weather. They asked me what I thought was going to happen. I stated, "These storms always change course one way or the other at the last minute, and the news media always blows these things out of proportion. I wouldn't worry about it."

Boy was I wrong…

I was dead wrong…

After a cordial Adieu' to the impromptu storm-watchers group, I went back across the street and told Dave that we would check the weather in the morning, and if there was indeed a storm coming, we would board up the windows on the beach side of the motel, but I was not going to evacuate. The next morning, the storm was still projected to make landfall at Mexico Beach. We boarded up the windows, and then I bought some steaks for dinner, preparing to stay in the apartment behind the office. By late afternoon, the city was a ghost town, and the police came to urge me to leave. I thought that I might as well go, (I needed a day or two off anyway), so I grabbed some clothes and one of my laptop computers and put them in my car, leaving my truck behind in the parking lot.

I drove to Tallahassee and checked into a motel room.

The next morning I awoke to news reports that the storm had strengthened to category 4 status, and the eye was about 4 hours away from landfall at Tyndall Air Force Base, the strongest winds of the rotation coming directly over the little town of Mexico Beach.

The rains and winds were whipping profusely, electrical transformers exploding in the distance, as I watched helplessly at the radar.

Hurricane Michael arrived as a category 5 hurricane, inflicting a direct hit on the little motel, washing it out to sea.

And just like that, it was gone…

Michael was the first Category 5 hurricane on record to make landfall in the Florida Panhandle.

First Report

October 13, 2018
(Posted on social media)

    Cellular telephone transmissions have just been restored in the Tallahassee area. It is with a heavy heart that I must report that Hurricane Michael has destroyed the Buena Vista Motel, as well as most of the City of Mexico Beach. It seemed to come out of nowhere, inflicting a wrath of devastation the likes of which I never could have imagined. Please keep us in your prayers, and remember that material objects mean little in this world, and that Love and Faith conquers all.

Michael reached its highest strength as a Category 5 hurricane with maximum sustained winds of 160 mph. on October 10, 2018, as it made landfall between Tyndall Air Force Base and Mexico Beach, Florida.

18

Dad, You Need to Write

October 12, 2018

The second day after the storm, I had returned to Mexico Beach to survey the damage. I then drove back to Tallahassee for supplies.

I was inside a large wholesale store, buying water, food, gasoline, and other needed supplies to maintain my existence at Ground Zero. I knew what the next few months there would be like, yet I had to return. I had to return to the place I loved the most. I had to help the others. My cell phone rang.

It was my son, Justin Michael, frantic to make sure I was alive. I reassured him I was okay, further explaining to him the details of what had happened. He then mentioned that my three grandchildren saw the news also, but were too young to understand.

My son rarely offers opinions, nor advice to anyone, myself included, so I was surprised at what he had to say.

I had the phone to my ear, while loading up the cart with cases of beanee weenies, when he spoke with a sincerity that I had rarely experienced from him.

"Dad, whatever you do, write everything down, every day, Write down what happened, write down what you are going through. Write down everything that happens."

I paused for a minute, looking at the bags of dry milk powder and bulk coffees, when he added, "Dad, you need to write."

Michael was the strongest hurricane ever to hit the United States during the month of October.

GROUND ZERO

"There is no sense of time; only dawn, heat, dusk, and dark."

Friday, October 12, 2018

    I received information that gasoline was available 26 miles away in Panama City. Three-hour drive on Hwy 98 through debris; massive devastation across Tyndall AFB, as well as through Callaway. Spent seven and a half hours in gas line; no food, no water.
    Witnessed forklifts dumping tons of food into dumpsters, most still refrigerated. Headed north on Highway 231 toward Interstate 10. Back to Tallahassee for supplies, arrived at 7:00 P.M. Central Standard Time.

Saturday, October 13
    Drove to a wholesale club in Tallahassee, bought generator, food and water, filled gas cans, and arrived back at Mexico Beach around 4:00 P.M., C.S.T. Shifted into mental autopilot, kept planning and working. Still no phone service. No communication with outside world.

Sunday, October 14
    Had three holes in tire from debris, walked to neighbor Jim's house, found tire plug kit, plugged tire. Procured construction trailer from a friend. Jim pulled trailer to mobile home, began removing items from house and storing. Reports of power being out for weeks or months.

Monday, October 1
    Drove back to Tallahassee on three sidewall plugs with fingers crossed to replace tire, cash checks, and get more gas. Bought solar lights.

Witnessed hundreds of emergency vehicles, power line trucks, National Guard, and law enforcement convoys in route.

Tuesday, October 16

Established base camp. Drove into Mexico Beach to Ace Hardware. Store destroyed. Obtained permission to enter building for plumbing fitting. Crawled under tumbled display racks; over paint cans to front of store, found PVC coupling. Repaired well pump, got water on, washed clothes by hand. Put up clothesline. Went to local church to help unload truckload of bottled water. Wasps and hornets everywhere.

Wednesday, October 17

Drove into Mexico Beach to survey damage and check on people. Procured MRE's and ice from coast guard units. Looter shot in Port Saint Joe. Dave went on ice run, met cadaver dog team members, reports of bodies in rubble in Mexico Beach; still two dozen residents missing.

There is no sense of time; only dawn, heat, dusk, and dark.

Thursday, October 18

Continued removing items from blown out mobile home residence. Placed gas stove from mobile home into construction trailer, hooked up gas bottle to cook meals.

Heat is unbearable.

Keeping eyes out for displaced snakes.

Exhausted, sleeping in room with partial roof gone, sweating.

Running generator ten minutes on hour to keep food safe in freezer. Mosquitoes emerged in force.

Witnessed examples of total selfishness and greed from a few individuals. Pity.

Reality begins to sink in.

Death toll reaches 19.

Experiencing moments of dazed confusion,

Unable to concentrate.

A wave of tears seems just on the horizon, praying to stay strong.

THE TWELVE DAYS OF MICHAEL

November 1, 2018

On the Twelfth day of Michael,
 FEMA gave to me;

Twelve cases water,
Eleven beanee weenies,
Ten bags of crackers,
Nine rolls of tissue,
Eight is the curfew,
Seven motel vouchers,
Six woolen blankets,
Five - Big – Blue – Tarps..........
Four Hygiene kits,
Three hot meals,
Two bags of Ice,

And a case full of M.R.E.'s

EVACUATION POST

In most regards, it seemed like a normal afternoon on the beach. The waves were rolling in gentle swells, coming closer, until they began breaking at the shoreline. It always seemed to me that each wave was attempting to come ashore if only to retreat, as the next one behind it made its own attempt. Then another came, and still another, in a constantly repeating rhythmic cycle.

There was a cool breeze coming in from the northwest, which was common during October. The only difference was that no guests were at the little motel. The stores were all closed, and there was little or no traffic to be seen. We heard reports of a large storm approaching from far off on the horizon, and most residents had chosen to evacuate.

After securing the trash cans in the storage room under the stairs,
I started placing the deck chairs inside the rooms. I thought about how many times we boarded up the windows in the past and left town while heeding warnings of storms forming far away, only to come back and take them down again. Most would remain tropical storms, and sometimes the surge would flood the little Tiki bar underneath the building,

"Oh no, not again," I thought.

I remembered how the seaweed and driftwood would wash up with the surges, and how much of a chore it was to clean it up afterwards.

I thought about Hurricane Opal, a category three storm, and how the storms surge had made the deck pilings sag.

"Dad gummit," I thought, "I might have to jack the decks back up again after this one." I went back into the office, meandered around the counter, then headed toward the laundry room.

There was a small refrigerator between the washer and dryer. Inside it, I had placed a nice rib eye steak. I opened a beer, and then set the steak on the counter to begin the marination process. Suddenly, there was a loud knock on the office door, and as I approached, the door opened.

I was greeted by two law enforcement officers, each from different agencies, yet both seemingly high in authority.

One officer said, "Mr. Kent, there is a mandatory evacuation procedure in effect. We urge you to evacuate immediately."

"No, I'm fine! I have food and water, and plenty of batteries!" I replied.

The second officer stated, "Sir, we cannot force you to leave. However, we will be closing the bridges soon, and you will have no way out after that."

I thanked the both of them for their concern, while reaffirming my stance on the matter. The two officers nodded, and turned away toward the stairs leading down to the parking lot. Just then one paused.

He turned around and said, "Could you do us one favor?"

"Sure," I responded.

He handed me what appeared to be a bold red permanent marker, as the second Officer asked, "Would you please write your full name in large letters on your forearm, just in case?"

The gravity of his comment shot through me, and I felt the hairs rise on the back of my neck. They were serious, and I could sense that they were indeed in fear for my life.

I raised my hand up, pointing my index finger at them, and said, "You know what? If you guys can wait about two minutes, I'm going to grab my laptop and a bag of clothes, and I will follow you out of here!"

I stuffed the computer, a few clothes, and the cans of beer in a duffle bag, then followed them down the stairs. I got in my car and drove away as they escorted me to the edge of town, where they stopped. I continued driving, while in my rear view mirror, I could see my little town slowly disappearing from my sight.

REAR VIEW MIRROR

There is a strange thing about a rear-view mirror; as you are driving away, the objects in your view become smaller and smaller. Our brains interpret that as distance, until they disappear from sight. I rolled the window down, glancing into the side window, and read,
"Objects in mirror are closer than they appear"
Nonetheless, I continued on my exodus out of the way of the storm's path, yet returned the day after. Like most survivors here, I endured the aftermath, and started over.
I witnessed so many incredibly strong people around me. I saw an outpouring of love and unity, and felt compassion and caring from everyone affected. The events of the past few weeks had united us all in an unspoken bond.
It reminded me of the mirror. Maybe the best things in life are *closer* than they appear.

28

NATURES REFUGEES

I found myself in view of a large estuary on the bay side of Cape San Blas today. I took a long moment to simply watch the spectacle of the birds in flight, the fish hopping along out of the water, only to splash down again and carry on...The birds are plentiful here, as if to maybe be displaced from a home they had closer to the storm. The pelicans are large, just like the ones that resided at the canal in Mexico Beach. I admire their gentle flight in and out of the flats here...these guys are pros, they can fly a half inch over the surface, and then choose whether to skim the placid surface to a resting point, or regain lift, and head back up into the skies. A Large Bald Eagle flew higher than the rest, and my interests focused on him...Where was he nesting? Where did he come from? There was an Eagle in Mexico Beach that I have made note of in the past prior to the storm, and I am curious if he was the same one. The closer I get to the Wildlife and Nature, the closer I feel to God...Of all the photos and events that I witnessed in the aftermath of the storm, I had not seen any evidence of any wildlife deaths. They merely evacuated like us, and they are living in the bay side of the cape, where I am staying.

SCENIC ROUTE

One Day I was tasked with a trip from Port Saint Joe to Apalachicola, and was to be accompanied by a colleague driving another vehicle. When I gave him the directions, I stated that the road forks just outside of town, and merges back together just before our destination. I further explained that to the left was the main business highway, and to the right was what is called, "The Scenic Route."

He chose to stay to the left, and I chose the right hand lane. Once we reconvened on the outskirts of Apalachicola, I asked him what he saw. He stated nothing other than a long seemingly endless highway, with row after row of planted pines flying past his peripheral vision. Then he turned and asked me, "What did *you* see"?

I responded, "I saw a beautiful coastline lay out before me while I drove along the shoreline. I witnessed large white cranes perched diligently in the shallow waters; a flock of geese cruising in for landing, followed by a patrol of pelicans. Then, around the bend, a large red fox crossed the highway in front of me. I was just far enough back to slow down and fully witness this beautiful creature. Further, around the bend, I arrived at Indian Pass, where the sun had begun to paint the sky in watercolor fashion. The birds were all flying in by this time, in order to shelter for the night in the shallow saw grasses. Around the last bend before the main highway, on the knoll of a wooded area, were three baby armadillos, munching along like rabbits."

This really happened that day. I wanted to share it with everyone on this Christmas Eve and remember that life is beautiful. Always take the scenic route.

BEACH-HENGE

For centuries, scientists, historians and scholars alike have contemplated the mystery of Stonehenge. What was it? Through modern analysis, the mystery has finally been solved; It was a beach house that was hit by a really big storm.

SAINT JOSEPH'S SEA DRAGON

I believe it came from the deep sea, just off the gulf shoal.

Quite possibly, it had been swept from its lair by the forces of the hurricane. Apparently displaced, I spotted him and caught this photo. Behold, the Saint Joseph Sea Dragon.

34

THE NEW NORMAL

Hurricane Michael was so pivotal of a moment in our lives that to a lot of us, for the rest of our lives, will refer to events as "Before the storm" or "After the storm." These are a few of the lessons it has taught me so far...

Rules for living in the new normal:

1. Do not get in a hurry. For anything.

2. Do not think nor expect things will go your way. Ever.

3. Always remember that electricity, running water, and the garbage men taking your trash away are a blessing, not a right.

4. Fully accept the notion that "It is what it is."

5. Remember that money can never replace what you think you lost.

6. See others and yourself as if we were all in the same lifeboat.

7. Choose sharing over hoarding.

8. Remember that "less is more" and that material objects, debt and worry can weigh down the soul.

9. Take care of your health and body. It is the only real possession you have.

10. Try to find peace.

36

HIS NAME WAS HOWARD

    I was a young teenager working in my father's furniture store. Howard had asked my dad for a job, and for the next two years or so, I would walk uptown from school, and Howard and I would deliver pieces of furniture, console televisions, and appliances to folks in our small town. He was always smiling, and we had fun together.
    What a strange coincidence that thirty years later, I would purchase a small, six room motel on a little beach, some eighty miles away, and he and his wife would happen to own a beach house next door. We would laugh about the old times, and he would tell me of his many adventures as a motorcycle police officer; a position he took after our days at the furniture store. He and his wife would travel down on the weekends, and he would always come up to my office to look for me. Sometimes he would bring me gifts, other times he would just come in to say hello, and shoot the breeze, but he always came looking for me.
    He would often bring me a bag of tomatoes, and tell me, "Now, those are Gadsden County tomatoes right there! They are the best tomatoes in the world!" I always agreed, and he would smile from ear to ear with pride.
    Then he would add, "I love them on a mater sandwich," and proceed to tell me exactly how to make one, "You just put a big slice on some white bread, spread some mayonnaise on it, and sprinkle a little bit of black pepper."
    "It's better than a steak dinner," he would say.
    I would laugh nodding, because he had told me that every time he brought me tomatoes. Howard was getting on in years, but every time he came to his beach house, he would come find me to visit. He knew that I played guitar, and one day he came into the office.

    "Hey Michael, I want to show you something," he said. He was beaming with pride, as he held up a six-string guitar.

        "I'm going to learn to play it," he said. "I've always wanted to."

I found myself equally excited for him, and he insisted I play it for a moment. He was like a little kid in a candy store over that guitar. For the many months that followed, I would find myself walking around the decks of the little motel, and I would hear singing. I would walk to the edge of the deck facing the beach, and Howard would be sitting in a chair next to the dunes, his gospel music book in front of him, strumming away and singing hymns. I would smile, and I could see he was in total joy with it.

It was the end of September, and one day he came to office to find me. He held out a large hunk of watermelon.

"I wanted you to have half," he said, as we laughed and talked. "These here are Gadsden County seedless watermelons". He commented, followed by "They don't have any seeds". I would nod in agreement, offering a look as if I had just learned something fascinating. As our visit came to an end, he turned toward the office door, and headed down the stairs.   "Okay Mike, see ya later," he said as he waved to me. That was the last time I saw him. I got a phone call informing me that he had passed away from an aneurysm in his garage in Gadsden County, as soon as he got home.

Two weeks later, Hurricane Michael destroyed the little motel, and Howard's beach house as well. There was nothing left of them except a few broken pilings and concrete slab fragments. For what seemed like an eternity, I stood by the edge of the highway, looking over the remains of what once was. I found myself speechless, confused, and overwhelmed by how surreal everything appeared.

How strange of a notion, to think that the last time we stood out on the deck and told a few jokes, we had no clue that in two weeks, everything around us would be gone, non-existent, and that Howard himself would be gone too.

Please take the time to see the fragile beauty in this life, embrace it, live every day as a gift; live it to its fullest. Tell people you love them, and when you hug someone, be the last to let go. Try to find Peace.

BUENA VISTA MOTEL
INFORMATION AND POLICIES

903 Highway 98, Mexico Beach, Fl. 32410
Office (850)-648-5323
Emergency # (850)-866-9397
WIFI code: 903mexicobeach
No Smoking allowed in rooms
Check out 10:00 AM c.s.t.
Extra parking available across the street to the left of gulf foods.
   Towel exchange-return used towels to the office between
9-12 am in the white basket provided. If the office
is locked, leave it at the door, we will deliver it to your door.
   Please be aware of Mexico Beach "Leave No Trace"
Ordinance -Anything left on the beach 7pm-7am
will be removed.
   Please do not use Motel items on the beach: towels, white baskets, chairs, etc...
   Additional room charge for more than 2 people over 10 years of age.
NO PETS

Due to events of the past, as well as recent occurrences in this regard, I submit the following commentary. Your comments are welcome, as well as encouraged......
   The Buena Vista will no longer allow pets.
Pets include Dogs, (canines), Cats, (felines), any Marsupial, reptile, amphibian, or rodent.
We also shall not harbor Birds or Monkeys of any kind.
Pet rocks are ok.

   Please, no freaking Elephants or giraffes. The decks won't hold the Pachyderms and the giraffes are peeking into the rooms above theirs..
So please...Leave your bats in their Belfry, The dogs on the porch,

and the cats in their sandboxes;
That is where they are the happiest. You may love the beach, but they don't. Stop being selfish.

Any inhabitant simply must be Human. (Homo sapiens, Neanderthal and Cro-Magnon are accepted). Homo erectus subject to manager approval. DNA kits are available at the front desk, free of charge, (If needed for clarity).

Please do not throw cigarette butts off the decks into the sand. It may seem convenient for you, but the ghost crabs have taken up smoking and we are trying to get them to quit. Some of the seagulls have been swallowing them as well. Please refrain from discarding plastics or trash of any kind on the beaches. Fishing line, straws, etc. can kill Sea Turtles, birds, and other wildlife. This beach is an amazingly complex and beautiful ecosystem, and it is a privilege for us to be able to interact with it.

So Please, Take only photographs and memories, and leave only footprints........

AFTER THE TEMPEST

We spend too much time sifting and searching through the rubble, when if we let it go, we might just find "ourselves"...

To be a storm survivor, is...

To witness your physical world destroyed by the forces of nature;
To feel anguish, despair, and despondency cut deep into your inner core;
To find strength through unyielding faith;
To learn to adapt to a new reality;
To improvise with what few resources were left available to you;
To humble yourself to a new beginning...

But most importantly,

To succeed against the most stringent of odds;
and to rise above the rubble;
becoming far stronger than you ever
Imagined you could be...

Sand Castle courtesy of Raleigh Satterwhite

CASTLES IN THE SAND

Today I found myself looking through photos from two summers ago, and found one of a sandcastle that had been sculpted by a guest at the little motel. I remember he spent hours working with the sand, placing it in buckets to saturate it with water in order to make it firm, and then sitting under his canopy while sculpting.

Many times over the years, I would see children go down the stairs with their little buckets and shovels, spending hours building little sand castles of their own. The next day I would walk around the back deck, and notice their creations collapsing as they washed out to sea. It was inevitable that Mother Earth would reclaim them. However, it mattered not to the sculptors what tomorrow might bring, for they found joy while living in the moment, most often returning to build yet another one.

As I reminisced, the photo took on a new meaning to me. I realized that in essence, I had done the same thing as they, only on a larger scale. The little motel on the beach was symbolic of my own sand castle; I spent my days there sculpting it into what it was, while finding joy like I saw in those children's eyes. I lived for the moment, without the fear of imagining what the future might bring. And just like the little sand castles on the beach, one day Mother Earth reclaimed it, and washed it out to sea.

Yet the beach, in all its beauty, was still there. I knew then what I must do. I should follow the example of the children. I should grab my bucket and shovel, and build me another one.

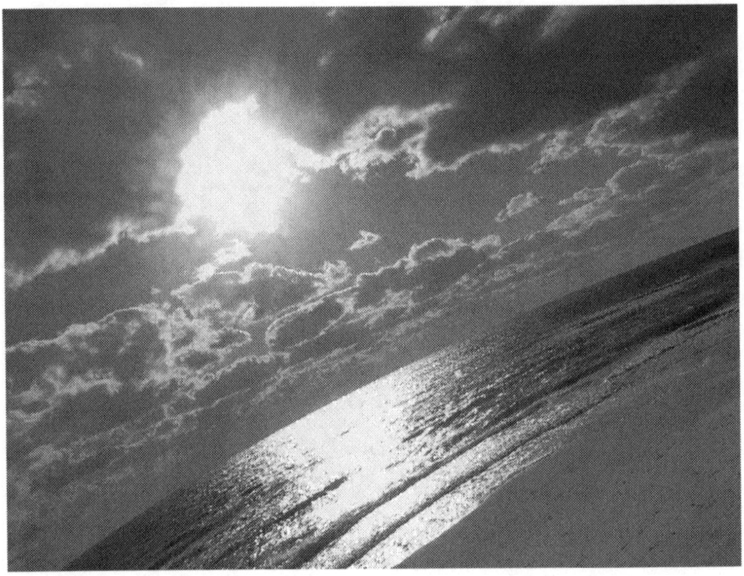

SPACESHIP EARTH

It seemed like the most popular time of day was just before the sunset. Guests and friends would always gather on the back deck in anticipation of it. It was not necessarily the setting of the sun itself, which signals the end of another day that attracted them, it was also a visual masterpiece. The sun beaming through the horizon would illuminate colors of all spectrum, and would interplay with the clouds and currents, always changing, as if to be a live feed from God's canvas.

Many times, folks would comment to me about how much they enjoyed watching the sun go down.

"What do you mean, go down?" I would ask.

They would reiterate how the shiny orb would slowly fall in the sky, and then seem to disappear in a hurry, beyond the horizon.

Often, I would challenge them on their perception, and ask them to consider looking as far left along the horizon as they could see, then slowly follow it as far as they could see to the right. There was an obvious curvature in the fine line that separated the sea from the sky, and one could easily imagine that we were standing on a round orb ourselves.

"The sun did not go down." I would offer, "We are rotating away from its light."

Life is all about our perception of it. The universe simply does not revolve around us. So when it's time for the next sunset, grab on to the handrail and hold on, while you witness our little planet orbiting around in our little solar system, on our never-ending trip around the sun.

46

The Ninja Chronicle

One of the most magical things to me about the little motel on the beach was how people were constantly drawn to it as I was. It seemed to be a place of subtle transition between the noisy confusion of life and the gentle calm of nature. It was the place that worries and stresses seemed to disappear for most, including myself. The pelicans cared not of manmade woes as they glided overhead, nor did the dolphins as they swam just offshore. They were God's living creations, existing in pure harmony with the earth, the ocean, and the seemingly endless sky.

One day, a few guests were out on the back deck. Below them lie the sand dune, the natural barrier between the land and the shore. It hosted a root base of sea oat vegetation, where the sand crabs had made their homes. One of the guests came to find me.

"There is a rat on the beach! Do you have rats here?!" She asked frantically.

"No, Ma'am, but I will come take a look;" I replied.

I set the halfway folded towel down, and followed her out of the office to the edge of the deck.

"He was right over there," She stated, while pointing down toward a section of the dune fence.

"Ma'am, why that's no rat, that is a beach mouse;" I informed her, "They are a rare endangered species in some places, and part of the natural wildlife here."

The next morning, I spotted the little guy again. He had found his way up on the deck, and I caught him red handed, munching on a cheez-it cracker. I thought about what the consequences would be if he wound up in one of the rooms, and was sure that my "endangered mouse" or the "he's my pet" responses would not resolve the situation. I knew that I had no desire to kill it, nor could I bring myself to do that. I pondered for a moment.

"These mice don't know their boundaries. I should adopt a kitten, and raise it here. They will be aware of his presence, and stay away."

The next morning I found myself sitting in my truck, watching the train cars pass by. The crossbar lifted. I proceeded over the tracks, and then turned right. Down a narrow road through the woods lay the animal shelter. It was a large dome shaped structure, one could best describe as a "concrete igloo." I went inside, and just inside the lobby, was a large pen constructed of chicken wire, five feet wide, tall, and deep. There were two climbing posts inside, hosting a small platform on each. Also inside were fifteen to twenty mature black kittens, lying intertwined with each other, all sound asleep. It was a den of total feline laziness.

Suddenly, one of them shot out from under the lowest platform, hopping around on top of the snoozing residents. As they began to stir, he jumped up onto the first platform. He then looked down at the lethargic populace, his ears turning downward, and back, as if to replicate wings. He focused on them, choosing his next victims. He was indistinguishable from the others, except for his natural bobbed tail. He poised, then dove off of the platform, landing in the middle of the ongoing slumber party. One kitten raised its head, only for the attacker to bop his ears all about for a moment. He then turned to another victim, giving them a good ear bopping as well. When the punishment had been served, the perpetrator popped out his claws, and ascended the cage wire to the third platform.

I turned toward the reception desk, and announced, "Ma'am, I want this one, right here! He is a little Ninja!"

After passing a background check, I was allowed to take him home. I walked in the door with the mature kitten in one arm, while holding cat litter and food in the other. The first order of business was the litter box. I filled the plastic pan, and placed it in the bathroom. Then I placed the kitten in the litter box. He instantly showed me that he knew exactly what its purpose was.

Later that evening, I was lying on the bed watching television, when I had an eerie feeling that I was being watched. I glanced around, and saw the little night stalker peering out from behind a pillow. I tried to set up a defensive maneuver, but it was too late; as the fearless predator lunged forward in full attack mode, inflicting an ear bopping upon myself, just like the punishment his comatose compatriots received during his time in the pen.

Five days of attending to a litter box was five days too many. The next morning, I opened the office window, and fabricated a door for him.

"Ninja, outside is the world's largest litter box. Use it!" I decreed.

From that day forward, he would have free access to and from the beach, as well as around the little motel. He would stroll around the decks, checking on things like a security guard. One day, I walked by a guest room, and the door was open. I saw Ninja chilling on the bed.

"Oh, no, I apologize!" I said to the guests.

"Don't be silly! We love him!" They responded. The two little girls asked me if Ninja could spend the night with them in their room. Usually, when guests were checking in, Ninja would hop on the counter, demanding attention. If his demands were not met, he would merely lay on top of our paperwork, so we could not continue our transaction. Every morning, he would be at the door, after working the "Midnight shift". I would let him in, and he would sleep on my desk, while I worked. He had a towel all of his own to nap on, and I made sure that it was in proper order at all times.

At the bottom of the stairs behind the little motel was a large sand dune, creating a natural buffer between the small inn and the surf. Ninja had found a special spot, just before the cusp of the knoll, where he would nestle in among the sea oats, and stare out toward the beach. One day, I was looking out over the back deck, when I saw the little beach mouse scurrying through the sea oat foliage. He was right next to where Ninja was on the dune.

I thought, "Oh my, he is going to kill that mouse."

The mature cat cared not about the mouse. It was not a threat to him. He merely watched the tiny rodent scurry along on its way, and then turned his attention to nature's next visual presentation, perhaps two sand crabs jousting with one another, or a seagull performing aerial maneuvers for a French fry wielding tourist…

For the next ten years, this amazing animal and I would share a bond; a friendship that I cannot describe in words. His demeanor was admirable, his intelligence obvious, and these traits that he carried were apparent to all others that encountered him.

One morning, I noticed that he was not standing by the office door, as he did every morning. I opened the door, to glance across the deck in search of him.

It was then that I saw him. I ran down the stairs, past the

parked cars, to the grassy area adjacent to the highway. I picked up his lifeless body, and cradled it while I climbed back up the staircase. I heard people speaking to me, but I could not acknowledge them. I was in a trance of sorts, in a form of shock. I laid my Ninja on his napping towel, and gently bundled it up. I walked down the stairs to the beach, as waves of emotion came over me. The first one was of anger, then confusion, then sorrow, each one coming and going like the waves on the beach. As I started digging in the sand; my eyes filled with water. As I dug, I would blink, and the water would run down my cheeks. I buried my best little friend under his favorite spot in the world, just behind the cusp of the knoll, on the sand dune.

THE SMALLEST PERCENTAGE

The washing machine was running constantly, accompanied by its sidekick, the dryer. I got used to the sounds they made, as it was another part of the routine of operating the little motel. People would come, and people would go. The phone would ring, and we were always folding towels. Most of the human visitors to the beach estuary were appreciative and kind to the environment, but there was a small percentage of the humans that I encountered, that had no apparent regard for living things, nor the planet that hosted them. These are the true stories of events that occurred throughout my tenure at the helm.

It was early spring, and my friend Claire and I were cleaning rooms around the little motel. As I walked out onto the back deck, I glanced over past Howard's house to the vacation home on the other side. There was a group of young boys, maybe nine or ten of them, up on the top deck. They were feeding the seagulls, and had attracted a large flock; the birds flying close in and over the boy's heads, in competition for the next Chee-to or French fry. Then, in an instant one of the boys pulled a short flagpole out of its holder, placed it back on his shoulder, and swung the pole like a baseball bat. The weapon struck one of the birds with such force, that feathers flew off the creature as it fell, landing lifeless on the edge of the dune. I loudly exclaimed, "Do NOT do that again!

"The seagulls had retreated away from the boys, who had all looked over at me, then ran inside the house. I turned back into the motel room and told my helper Claire what had just transpired.. She happens to be a marine biologist, and she was instantly as upset as I was. I walked down the stairs to the beach, heading toward the stricken seagull.

As I arrived, I looked down to see that the bird had indeed perished. I glanced up at the house, and it looked like the mischievous young boys were peeking at me through the blinds. As I

walked back toward the little motel, I saw a female wildlife officer drive up, meeting Claire at the residence. "Oh boy" I thought, "Those boys are about to get it, and get it good!"
After a half hour or so, they returned, informing me that those boys would not so much as swat a mosquito anymore.

A couple checked in for the weekend. It was midafternoon, and my helper and I were servicing a room on the top deck, facing the beach. The man that had checked in earlier was out on the beach fishing and I saw him get a bite. He reeled in a large ray, dragging it up on the beach. Rays are very interesting creatures, so I watched him take the hook out of its mouth, and presumed the next thing I would see was him place the ray back in the water, as they are of no use for food, nor bait. What I did see was him walk away and resume fishing. I said to my helper, "He's not going to put him back."

It was a reasonably hot afternoon, and the man continued to cast his pole, while the ray lay in the sun drying out, its wings flapping up and down, in its last desperate attempt at survival. I walked out of the room and down the staircases, heading to the beach. By the time I was over the dune, I could see it had ceased moving.

I turned to the man, and all I could say was, "You weren't going to put him back?"

I kneeled down, running my hands under the ray's belly, and carefully escorted him back into the water. His skin was dry, and he was unresponsive. After a few moments, he revived, and swam away back into the sea.

I was driving from Port Saint Joe and had just passed Toucans restaurant, when I saw a seagull lying in the center of the highway. It appeared that is was certainly deceased, as it lay there disfigured. As I passed, I thought I saw movement. I did, I saw it move. I pulled over, and ran to the middle of the highway, waving to divert traffic around us.

The large seagull was lying amongst a handful of French fries. Some idiot had thrown them out, and this innocent bird was going to die for just being hungry. I saw life in its eyes, so I pulled off my shirt, and reached down, wrapping him up. I placed the bird in my truck seat, and drove to the little motel, where I took him downstairs to the beach. A few guests had a canopy set up, and I showed the seagull to them. We dug a small depression in the sand under the shade of the canopy, and gently tucked his wing back in place. He was becoming more alert, because he began nipping at me in defense. Suddenly, he jumped up, began flapping his wings and regained enough lift to catch a wind current. He then flew away through the sunset.

Just beyond the back deck was the large dune, a swale of sand, sea oats, creeping vegetation, and the habitat of the sand crabs. The crabs had little pigment, almost clear, because they lived in small burrows they had dug into the dune, and came out mostly at night. You could see their tiny tracks in the sand, going from one hole to another, like they were visiting each other.

A family had two rooms on the lower beach side deck. The guest list included five or six children, who were in full beach mode, running around and having fun. They had inflatable balls, sand buckets, and little nets for beach toys. The sky had become dark, and I saw the parents had given them flashlights to go with their nets, in order to go exploring on the beach.

The next morning, I walked down the stairs to the back deck. None of the guests were there, it was midmorning, and I thought they might be at a restaurant.

On the edge of the deck in the open sun was a clear plastic container with a colored lid, somewhat smaller than a gallon of milk. The children had caught the sand crabs the night before, and filled the container to the top with them. I immediately pulled the lid off, to see maybe two dozen or so of the little creatures packed inside, the ones on top trying to get out, while the ones on the bottom that had seemingly accepted their fate, lay still.

"My God, they have been in the sun for hours now!"

They were not far from death, so I ran down the stairs to the dune, turned back under the deck to the shade, and laid the container on its side, gently shaking them out onto the cool sand. I glanced around and saw cigarette butts, wrappers, and beer cans laying among the sea oat vegetation. I shook my head in disbelief, as I procured a water hose from the tiki bar.

I focused back on the crabs, and thought to myself, "This is probably the entire population of the dune."

Three walked away. Some were upside down, and not moving. I gently turned them over, and gave them a gentle shower to cool them off. In the course of an hour so, each one regained consciousness, and found its way to one of their little caves in the sand.

"Lord, forgive the humans, for they know not what they do," I mumbled.

HE'S NOT MY DOG

The day-to-day operations at the little motel had become a routine lifestyle; Weekdays, weekends, holidays, or any-days did not change things much. Guests would come and go in random pattern, evolving into what I considered to be a normal flow. Comfort was found in the routine; it was constant, steady, and rarely changing. I compared it at times to the daily routine of the beach estuary; in a never-ending cycle, the sun would rise, carry on with its day, then set again.
      There were also times needed away. I would secure the fort, and drive up to Overstreet, where I had a modest mobile home on an acre of land. The pines were tall, the fruit trees plentiful, and the plants abundant. There I could find solace in writing songs, singing, and playing my guitar.
      It was a cold January afternoon, and I had settled into the studio, when I heard a scuffling noise outside. I opened the door, only to see a small puppy looking up at me. He instantly shot off of the porch, and began running toward the road.
      "Hey, Buddy!' I hollered, "Where ya goin?"
      The animal paused, and slowly looked back at me. He was no more than a few months old, but his paws had already outgrown him. He had no collar, yet he appeared to be in good health.
      I went back inside, and placed some leftovers on a plate. When I returned, the timid visitor was at the base of the porch steps. I laid the food down, and went back into the studio.
      The next day I arrived to see the furry transient sitting on the front porch.
      My friend Dave was with me, and said, "Looks like you have a dog."
      I responded defiantly, "He's not my dog!"
      I went in, rounded up a few more morsels from the refrigerator, and then placed them by the front door. Over the next

few days, I would arrive home daily to find the hairy little hobo awaiting my arrival.

I would shake my head, while heading into the kitchen. My life had been so hectic and confusing lately, that I had become frustrated.

I thought to myself, "He's not my dog.... I don't need a dog to keep up with."

The refrigerator yielded no fragments of meals prior, so I opened a beer and went into the studio.

The sound system came to life, and I started singing with my guitar as usual. Halfway through the song, I realized that the curious canine had wandered inside. He was watching me from around a corner, his head tilting slightly, as if in some form of awe. As I strummed the strings, his eyes grew larger. He cautiously approached, placed his paws up on my knee, and stared in wonderment at the instrument. I remembered a song from years ago, and began playing it for him.

"Feed Jake, he's been a good dog," I warbled.

The pup was mesmerized, and tried feverishly to get up on my lap.   Then I spoke, "You are not my dog!"

I put down the guitar, while beginning to doubt my stance on the matter.

For the next eight months, I would come home to him waiting on the front porch. I had resigned myself to buying larger portions of meats; and Jake and I would share in the bounty from the grill. Jake loved music, and he never missed a practice session.

It was the first week in October, and one day there was rumor of a tropical storm brewing far off on the horizon. The next day, the storm strengthened, and I was strongly advised to evacuate not only my residence on the shore, but also the mobile home among the trees. I threw a few articles of clothing in a bag, drove out of town toward Overstreet, with a police escort following me to the city limits. The roads were empty for the most part.

The skies were overcast and still. As I pulled into the driveway, I thought it odd that Jake was not on the porch, nor running toward the car as had been the norm. I went inside, thinking that I may have not let him out that morning. I walked around the yard, calling to him, with no response. There was an eerie sense of impending danger in the air, and I reasoned that he must have sought shelter in the dense forest. I circled the block, returned, and repeated the search again, but to no avail. I was forced to trust my instincts that he had found a protective burrow among the trees. The next morning, I awoke in Tallahassee, and turned on the television.

For the next five hours or so, I watched the storm of a lifetime pass directly over the little motel, and the trailer in the woods as well.

The next morning, I began the journey back. A drive that took an hour and a half the day before, took eight and a half to return. The day was spent navigating fallen trees, power lines, and roadblocks. Convoys consisting of Coast Guard detachments, law enforcement troupes, ambulances, heavy equipment, and power line trucks took precedent, as we slowly inched our way home.

Finally, I arrived at the bridge that passed over the community where the little mobile home was. The dense forest that cloaked the neighborhood was gone. I could see below, and the destruction was immense.

I navigated the car around the fallen trees, stopping at the entrance to the driveway. The tall pines were all broken over, the fruit trees uprooted, the plants obliterated. Debris was scattered everywhere, and the roof to the mobile home was gone. I got out of my car, and in somewhat of a trance, began walking toward the door, only to find it gone as well. I shouted out, "Jake!"

Nothing.

"Jake!"

Still, no response.

My heart sank. I looked around at the destruction, and found myself more concerned about him than anything else.

I shouted out again, "Jake! C'mon boy! I got steak!"

My attempt at bribery struck me as futile, while I braced myself for the realization that he had perished in the storm. The nicknames I had given him came to mind. Silly Dog, Clumsy Oaf, Big Lug. It is a strange feeling to be laughing and crying at the same time, but there I was, doing just that.

The next lapses of time are slightly unclear to me now. It could have been seconds, or it could have been hours. I just stood by my car, looking at the sky, feeling totally numb. My trance was broken by a rustling noise coming from the rear of the yard. My lost companion emerged from the woods, heading straight toward me. His right rear leg was swollen, and he was limping painfully.

"Jake!" I exclaimed. He lifted up his wounded appendage,

and shifted into a full three-legged gallop. It was then that I was knocked to the ground in a full body tackle, followed by a good flogging from an overly wagging tail. I am convinced the furry fullback was trying to lick me to death, but I did not succumb. Instead, I retaliated, by offering an equal punishment of belly rubbings and ear rufflings. We rolled around in the yard, wrestling in joy, while I was laughing aloud.

His name is Jake, and he *is* my dog.

THE REEF

    Over the years, I would find myself on many a countless afternoon, waiting for the laundry and tending to the telephone, while taking reservations for future visits to the little beach motel. I found out soon enough, that I could only play so many games of spider solitaire, so I shifted my mindless endeavors in the direction of the daily crossword puzzles. Intriguingly difficult at first, they too were soon mastered to the point of boredom. I then discovered that when I answered the calls, I would intuitively take to my pen, in anticipation of the next reservation...As the conversations unfolded, I would doodle along the edges of the pages...little fishes, swimming about.... One day, I drew a little balloon over one of them, and he had something to say.

So there I was, a grown man drawing cartoons.......

60

"THE REAL REASON FOR "SCHOOL OVERCROWDING"
FISHING BAN IN EFFECT
THE REEF

"THE REEF"
AND TODAY IN THE BALTIC SEA, NOTHING HAPPENED... AND TODAY IN THE CARRIBEAN, NOTHING HAPPENED... AND TODAY IN THE PACIFIC.....
"WATER CONCH-RITE"
NEWS "ANCHOR"
"NOT SO NEWS"
2-10

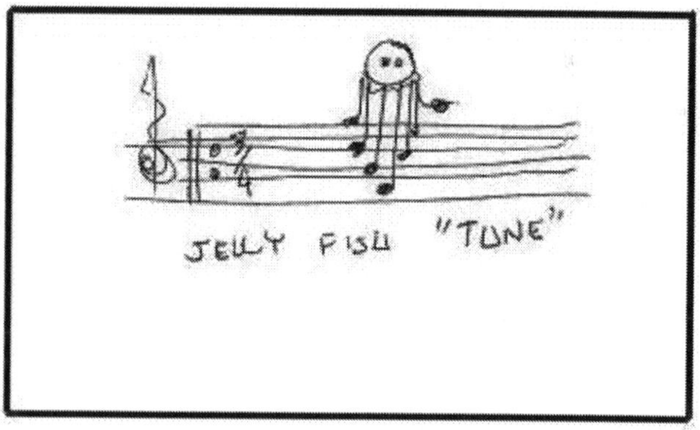
JELLY FISH "TUNE"

"Jellyfish Toons" featuring "Man-O-War"

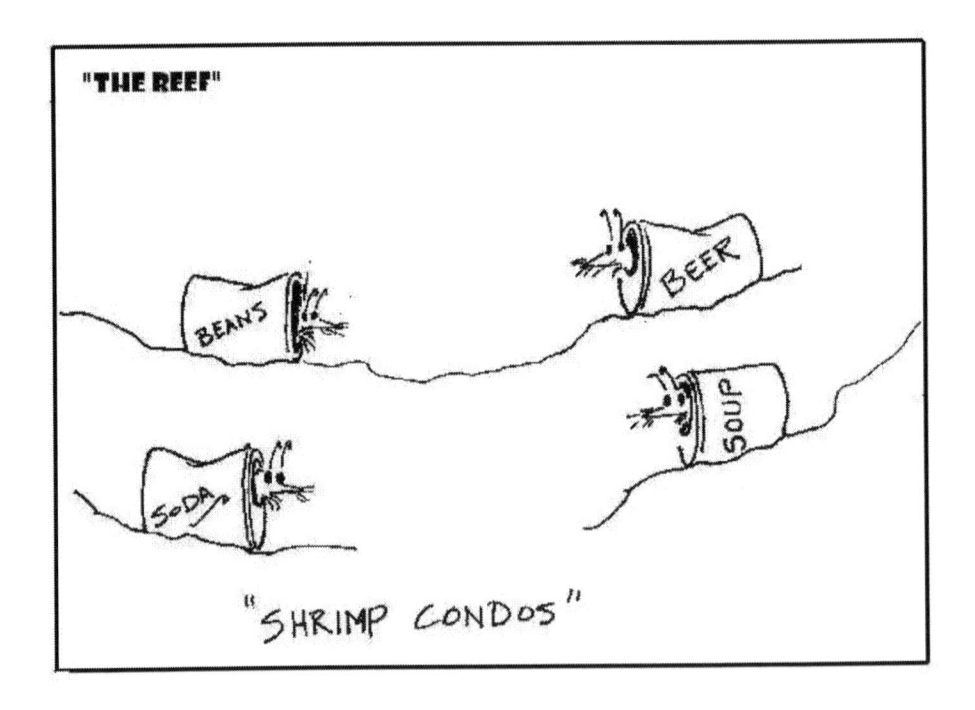

DESPITE WARNINGS... HAL CONTINUES HIS SUICIDAL ATTEMPTS TO...

REACH DA SOYFESS.

PITY....

The reef

"THE REEF"

BEANS

BEER

SODA

SOUP

"SHRIMP CONDOS"

"THE REEF"

Today will be "wet" followed by "wet"

"Meterological Jelly Weather Fish Guy"

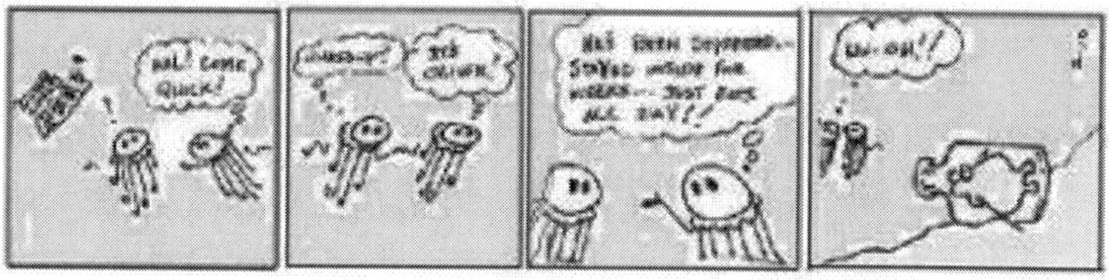

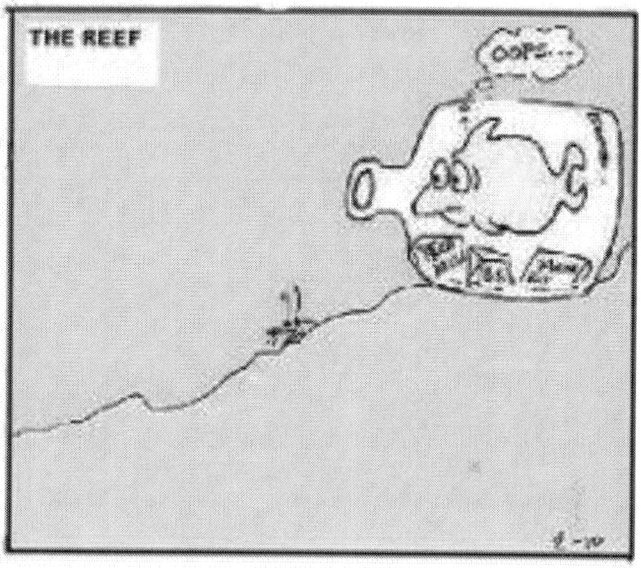
THE REEF
OOPS...

"THE REEF"

"FISH DIETS"

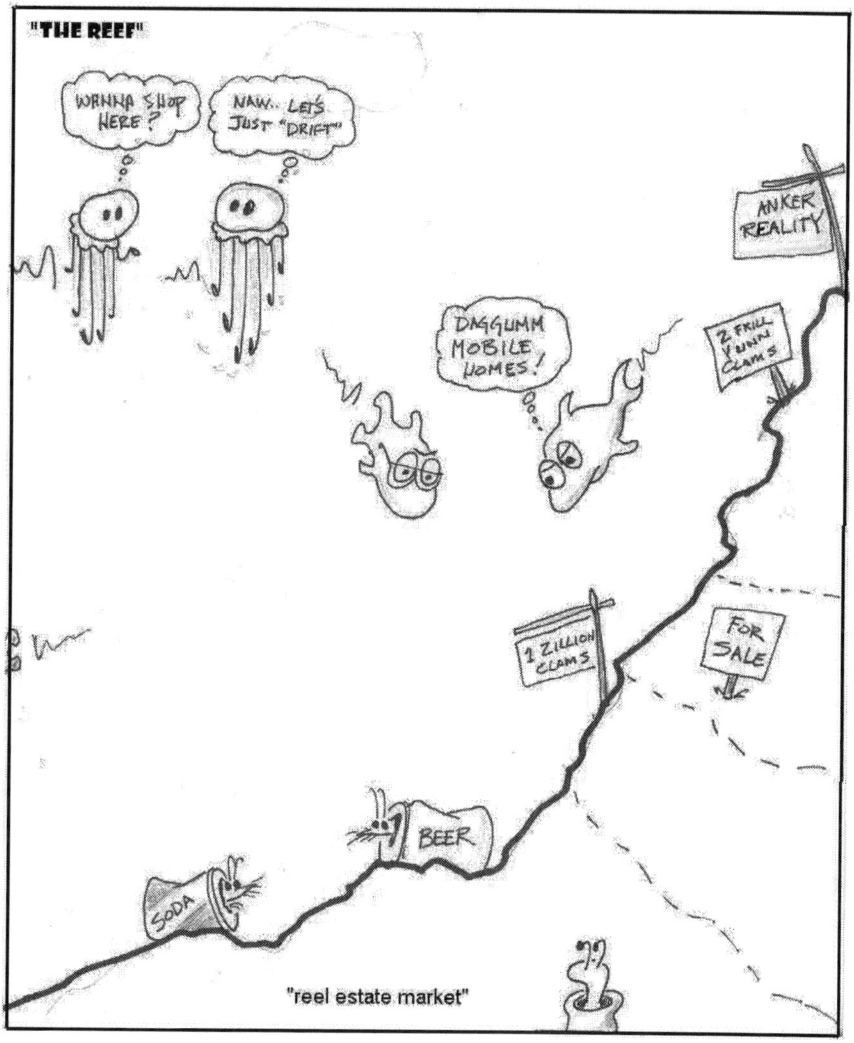

"reel estate market"

"THE REEF"

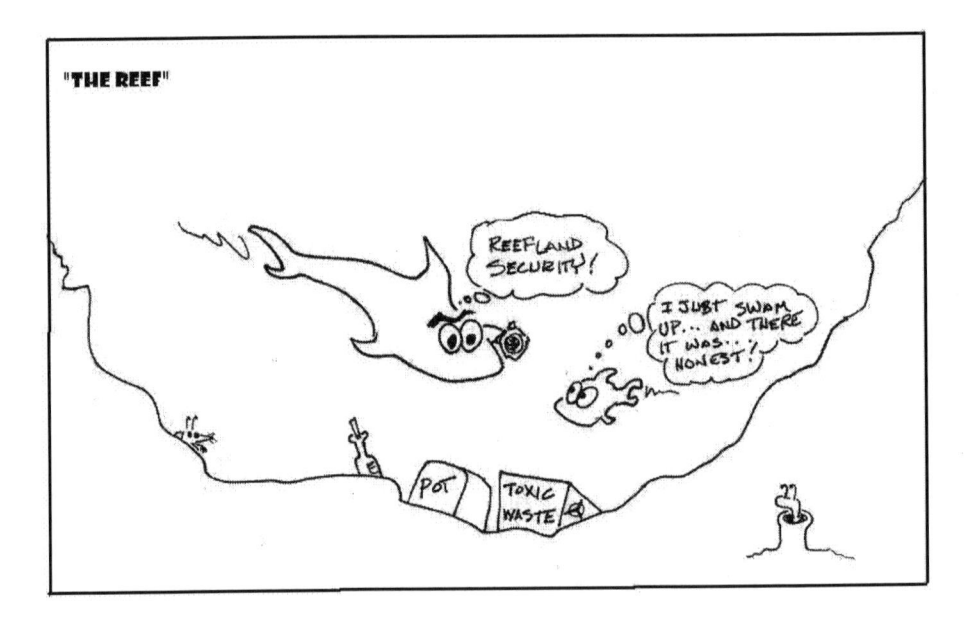

"THE REEF"

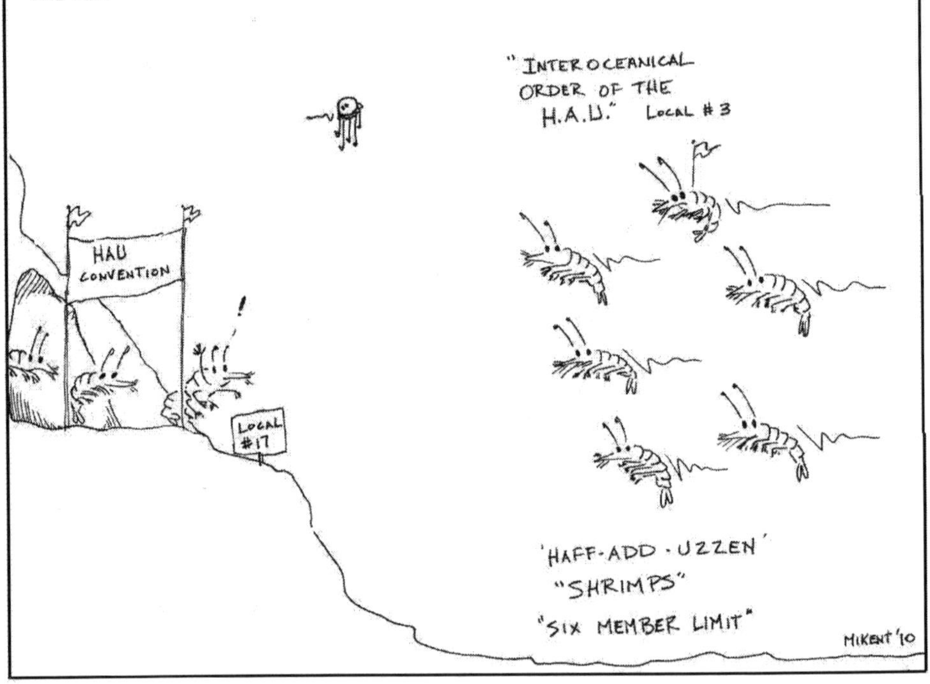

'THE REEF'

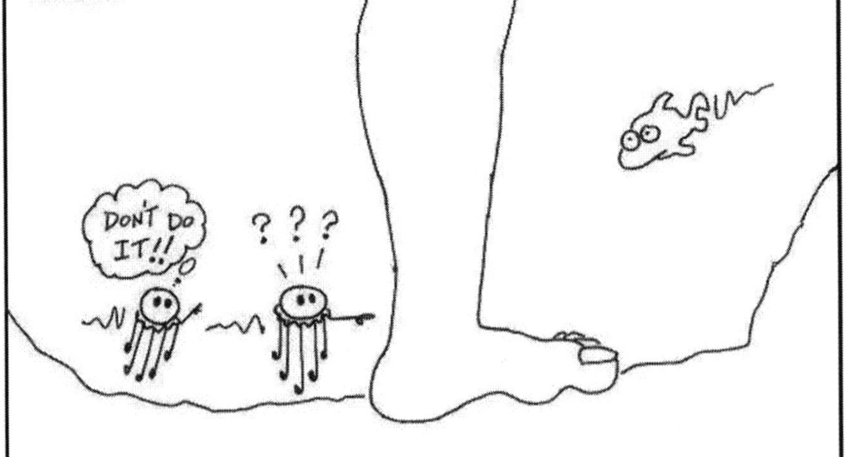

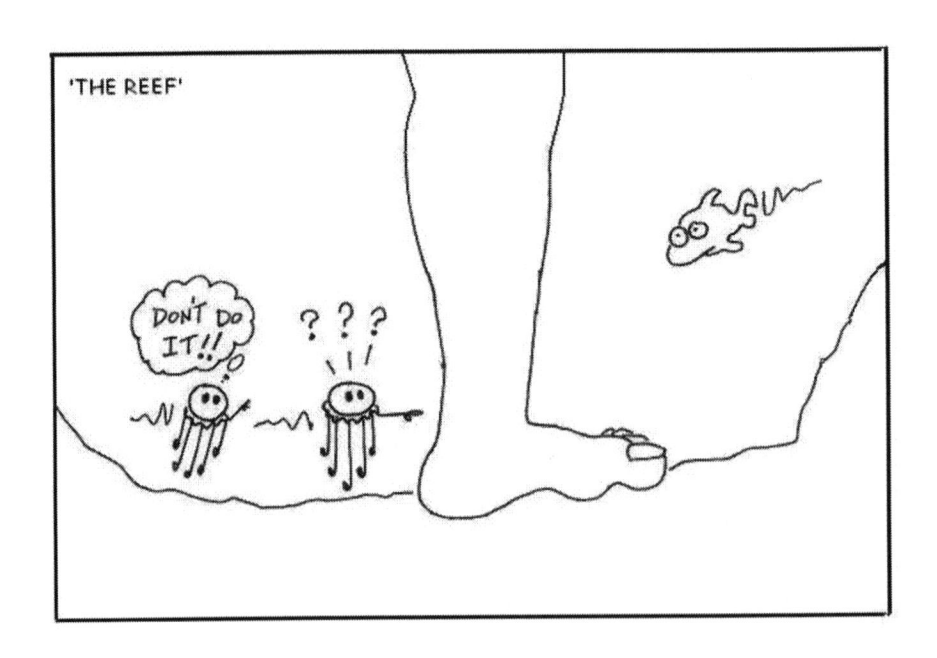

"THE REEF"

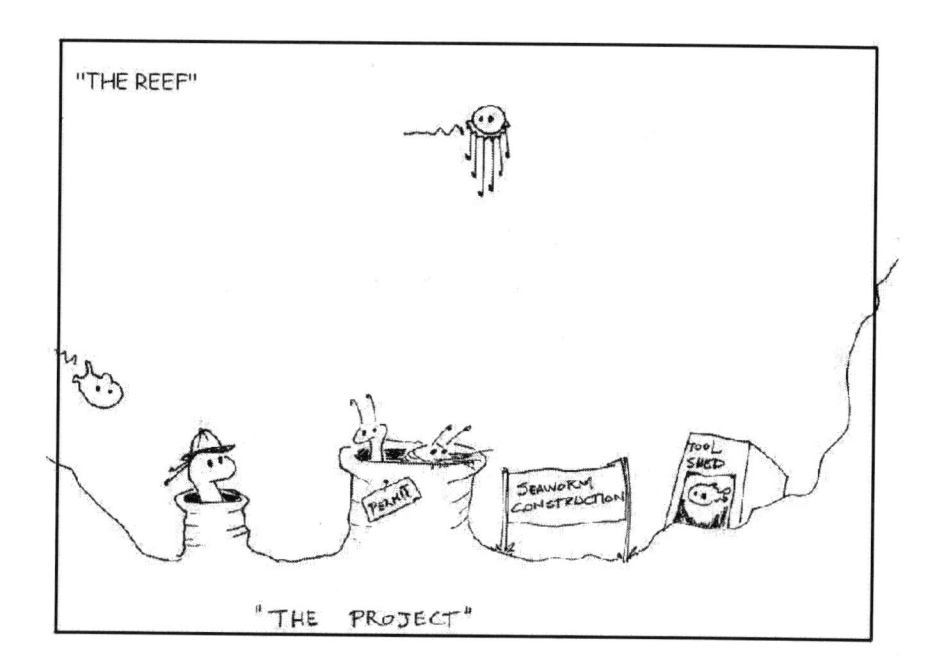

"THE PROJECT"

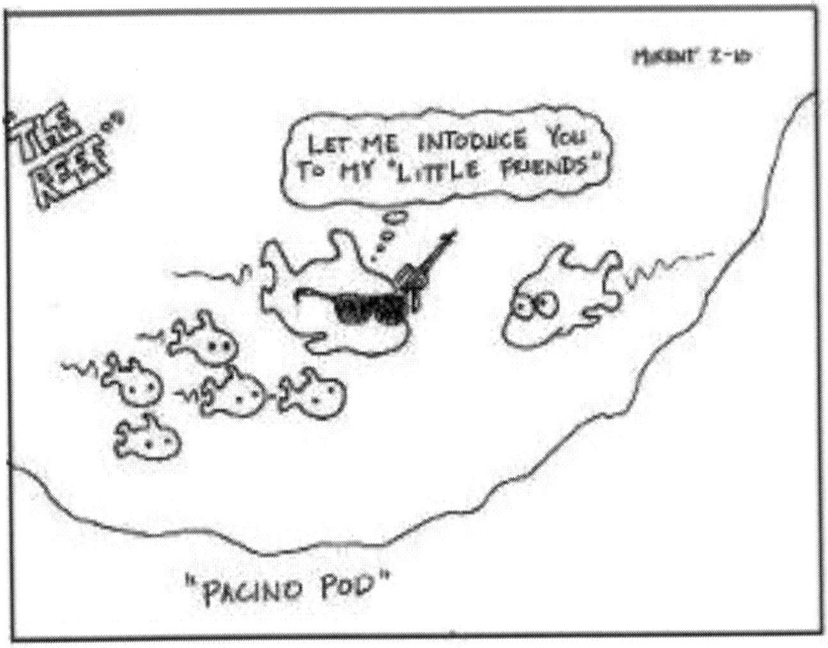

"PACINO POD"

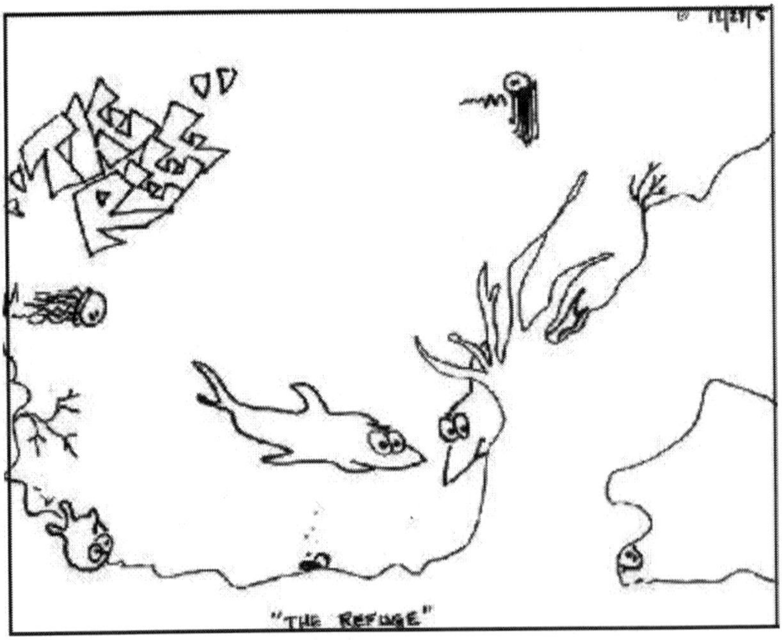

"THE REFUGE"

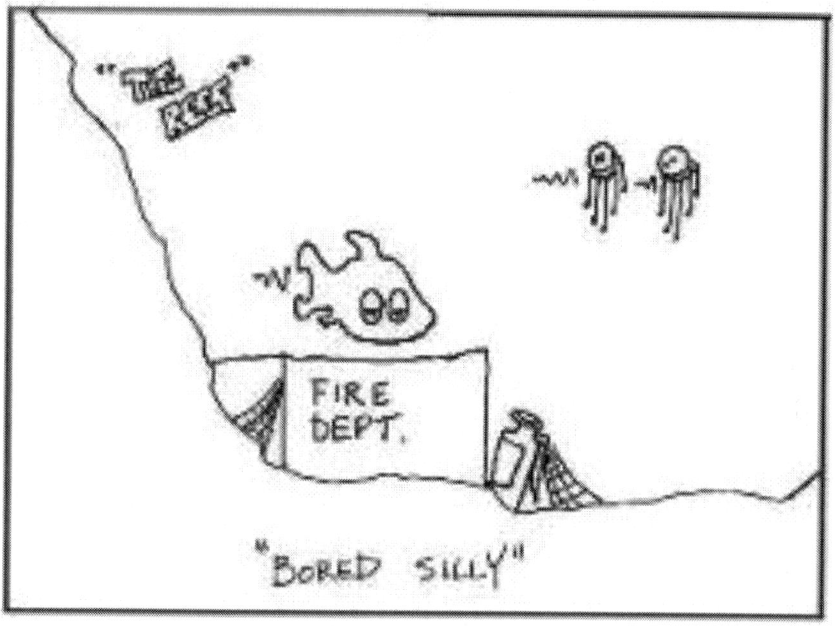

"BORED SILLY"

"Making Concessions"

"THE REEF"
HEY JACK! WHAT'S THAT?
OUR "INTERNET" SERVICE PROVIDER!!
MK '10

ANGELS AMONG US

One of the unforeseen aspects of the hurricane was the loss of tree density. The heat around ground zero was intolerable during the day, escalating quickly in the mornings, while producing heat indexes of 110-120 degrees on average. A friend of mine mentioned yesterday that he had to sit in the waiting room of the hospital yesterday for two hours. He described how wonderfully cool the air was in there; everyone was reading magazines, and it was quiet. I thought that sounded down right appealing.

The next afternoon, I left work, hot and tired, and went into town to buy supplies. As I rode by the hospital, I turned in. I walked into the lobby, then into the waiting area, and sat down. I felt the cool, clean air, yet said nothing. I looked over at the crumpled magazines haphazardly lying about, and chose one. As I sat there, a nurse came up to me.

"Are you looking for someone in particular?" she asked.

"No, Ma'am, I'm waiting for a phone call," I responded.

"Take all the time you need, sir. We will be here for you," she replied.

I could sense a love and caring in the air. I was chilling indeed. I instantly felt a twinge of guilt. I was bringing nothing to this table in exchange for my comforts.

Then I wondered, "Why am I even in here?"

I went back to my Readers Digest, and continued reading. After a few moments, a little girl walked up and sat down beside me. She was sitting on her hands, and her feet were swinging back and forth, while she was staring off into space.

"Hello". I said.

She glanced over, then looked back at the wall, while staring straight through it.

"My mommy is dying." she said.

I paused, and folded up the book.

"Hello, my name is Michael. What's yours?" I asked.

"Samantha," she said, as her voice trembled.

"Hey, you know what's so special about this place?" I asked.

She turned and looked at me inquisitively.

"Everyone you see here, loves your mommy, and wants to

make her well. And with all these people, the love is so powerful, I'm sure that your mommy will be okay."

I opened the magazine again, and began tearing out the key lime pie recipe.

"But what if she dies?" I heard.

I looked over, "You see, that's even the more special thing about this place. There are angels here, they walk among us. Why, there may be one walking by any minute." I said.

"How will I know if I see an angel, Mr. Michael?" she asked.

"Well, if you think you see one, you just wink at them. If they wink back, you found one."

I sat the book back on the table, and chose to just sit with my new friend for a moment. We found ourselves staring at a large clock on the wall.

A doctor walked in.

"Samantha?" she announced.

"Yes, Ma'am," was the reply.

"Baby, your mommy is doing just fine. Would you like to go see her?"

"Yes!" said the little girl, as the doctor took her hand and led her out of the waiting room.

Just as she turned the corner, the little girl paused. She looked back at me, and gave me a big wink.

I nodded, and winked back. She gave me the biggest smile, then she disappeared from my sight.

I felt then that there was a reason why I was there that day. Maybe something led me to that waiting room. Maybe not. Maybe I don't know, nor will I ever. But I did learn that the power of love is the strongest force on this planet, and that there are far more miracles among us than troubles.

THE VACATION MINDSET

As the seasons changed, so would the patterns of the visitors. Some preferred the cooler months, while others chose the warmer climates of Spring and Summer; some planning their beach time during holidays, while others visited at times in between them, as to avoid the crowds. Diehard anglers were always eager to come try their luck with a hook, while others were perfectly intent laying in the sun, swimming in the waves, or finding treasure in the many sea shells that lay abundantly about. Some would come to the beach as an escape, to find solitude, while others were hinging their plans around their children's time away from school. Nonetheless, the vacationers would always return to the beach. They would come from all lifestyles, nationalities, ages, and attitudes, but one thing seemed to be constant; the mutual attraction between the surf and the soul, an insatiable desire to return to the sea. Some favored the sunsets, seemingly mesmerized by the ever changing vistas, while others chose to stroll along the water's edge in the mornings, finding comfort in the stability of a calm surf. Some visitors would gather seashells, while others would find their happiness just being there, in the moment, with friends or loved ones.

There is a sense of renewal and replenishment one feels when embracing the ocean, and I regularly witnessed the strength of its healing powers. Travelers would arrive weary, or under stress, some feeling sadness or anger in their hearts, only to have their worries slowly dissipate like the waves at the water's edge.

One of the interesting facets of living in a reality of paradise, is the notion that there were still daily chores and duties to be done.

I accepted the tasks readily, stripping beds, churning laundry, and taking out trash. On busy weekends, it was not uncommon for the trash cans to fill quickly, often overflowing onto the sidewalk or parking lot, while waiting for the trash truck.

It was upon this dilemma that I forged a plan. A plan to forever rid the premises from the scourge of manmade refuse. I would build a wooden enclosure to house the containers and place it across the street at the rear of our overflow parking area next to the grocery store.

The structure consisted of wooden stockade fencing and long posts buried in the ground. One hot summer day, I opened the gated bin; my mind more focused on my imaginings than the task at hand, which was "taking out the trash." I was startled, as I looked down into one of the large garbage containers. At the bottom, trapped, was an elderly opossum. The animal had apparently been there for a day or two, a slave to the heat, with no water. His wrinkled skin soaked with sweat; his eyes reflecting the anguish and fear of accepting his fate; He knew that he was on the verge of death.

I pulled the container out, gently turning it over by the edge of the forest. The lethargic marsupial rolled out onto the ground. After a dazed moment, he slowly began to get on his feet, his shaky legs wobbling his sweaty frame back toward the path in which he came. The old possum stopped at the edge of the opening into the thicket. He turned around, and looked at me, our eyes connecting for a long moment. I could see a sense of appreciation on his face, as if to be thanking me for saving his life. He turned his aging eyes back toward the wood, then slowly meandered his way into the safety of the underbrush.

ANNIVERSARY RETROSPECT

Today, October tenth, marks the one-year anniversary of the day that Hurricane Michael arrived, and in a few short hours, changed the lives of many of us forever. I, as well as many other survivors, have spent the last 365 days in a seemingly endless state of shock, confusion, disbelief, and heartache. We found strength through resolve and perseverance, while learning how to perceive life in a new way, from a different perspective.

We have all engaged in discussions and opinions since then in our daily interactions, while across the internet, some of us have exchanged commentary, stories, reflections, and opinions on the topic.

Early on, I seemed to be having difficulty trying to grasp the reality of what happened. Occasionally, I would find myself lost in my thoughts; blindly staring off into space. We also had to deal with the random inquirers; the people we would see in public, at the grocery, hardware store, or gas station.

They would ask, "Hey, are you going to rebuild? What are you going to do?"

To them it might seem like casual conversation, or a greeting to show concern. But to those of us affected, it could feel invasive for them to do so. The inquisitors would ask broad, personal questions, forcing the respondents to repeat and relive the same dialogue, over, and over again, when all we really wanted was a loaf of bread, or a tube of caulk.

So as I reflect on the past year, I have decided to let it all go. I will cease to make Hurricane Michael the default setting for my discussions. I just don't want to talk about it anymore. It was in the past, and I am a survivor. I will file my remembrance of the storm in my memory bank, alphabetically, somewhere between "Harley" and "Husband,"

(When I had one, and when I was one.)

There is a reason that God placed our eyes and feet pointing in the same direction; He designed us to move forward. He also made it physically difficult for us to look or go back. He gave us life in the present, and the intelligence to understand the concept of a future; the hope of what lies ahead. He reassures the notion by having it arrive to us every second. So as I close this babbling retrospective rhetoric, I will share my most memorable random invasive question moment.

"That's not a bad price for those T-bones, I think I'll get some of those shrimp, and...

"HEY, DID YA LOSE ANYTHING IN THE STORM?"

I looked up startled, responding, "Oh, hello, _____" (fill in the blank)

"Well, it's kinda been like a Lost and Found," I replied, "First, I will tell you what I lost, and then I will tell you what I found. There was no insurance on the building, there is no money to rebuild; everything was destroyed."

I continued, "What I lost was a lifetime's worth of labors, material objects and assets, my retirement fund, my children's inheritances and grandchildren's college tuitions, a home, a truck, and a job.   The PA speaker interrupted my dissertation. "Clean-up in aisle three."

"Jeffery, please come to the service desk; Jeffery, to the service desk."

The intrigued inquirer responded; "But what did you find?"

I set the two steaks in the cart.

"What I found first was time and freedom," I responded. "Time to spend with my children now; time to invest my resources in them, rather than in inanimate objects; time to spend with my grandchildren; to teach them while they are young. I found freedom from the constant worrying over money and debt, and freedom from basing my measure of wealth and success in relation to material possessions."

"Then I found awareness. I became aware of how to see people for who they really were by their actions, rather than their words or social stature. I became more aware of the power of nature, and the resiliency of the human spirit. I discovered the joy of writing, as well as the time and freedom to do it. I became aware that money and objects mean nothing, and that I had traded my time and freedom away in pursuit of them."

I turned toward the glass counter, and pointed. "Could I get a pound of those jumbos?"

My impromptu interviewer exclaimed, "Wow! That's a great way of looking at things. Did you find anything else?"

I turned toward him. "Yes, I did. Most importantly, I found myself, and through that, I found peace."

"Clean up on aisle three!" blared the intercom, "Jeffery, to the service desk; Jeffery, service desk."

"Well, it's been good seeing you again Mr.Jones; Take care," I said. Suddenly, a short man in an apron waddled up to us, exclaiming, "Dammit, boy! If you don't hop to it, I am going to write you up!" My captivated interrogator looked at me again, and began removing his apron. He handed it to his overbearing employer, and told him, "I quit."

The little Luigi retorted, "Where are you going? You can't do that!"

And just like that, Jeffery Jones headed toward the door, and never looked back.

OMEGA MAN

It has been somewhat of a miracle to me, this new-found notion of writing; A pleasant means of escape on a moment's notice, to take the literary helm, and reason with myself, in a never-ending arena of possibility and conjecture...

Photo courtesy of Lacy Gray

It had been two weeks since the storm of storms. The surge of waste trucks, heavy equipment, and the process of the destruction of the destruction had begun, continuing in a seemingly never-ending cycle. One day the highway was closed off for construction, and for the six long months that followed, there was a detour around Ground Zero, in order to repair the bridge. I stayed the course, cleaning up and trying to rebuild something out of nothing while standing on a patch of sand.

The landscape had become a barren wasteland, reminiscent of science fiction movies I had watched as a young boy; The Omega Man, The Last Survivor. There was no traffic. There were no residents. All of the streets next to me were dead ends. I was cut off like the last man on the planet. I could find shade from the walls of the grocery store; the storm had surged in and washed away most of the contents, except for the grocery section to the right, where there was a brick stem-wall in front.

The property behind the store was once a forest. It had hosted bears, raccoons, armadillos, squirrels, and that pesky possum. The forest that had long flourished had been bulldozed and removed; I had seen no wildlife in quite a while. I wondered where they were.

The remains of the grocery store had a ghost like appearance, especially in the darker hours of the day. One day after firing up my charcoal grill, I took the notion to climb over the tumbled display case barricades, enter no man's grocery land, and procure a can of English peas. I was the Road Warrior.

I first climbed over the ice cream cooler, which was upside down, then over the dairy cases, carts, shelving, and debris, all thrown about. As I navigated toward the aisle where I knew the peas were kept, I found myself intrigued by the long center aisle; the image surreal, almost as if in black and white.

Slowly trekking forward, I noticed the broken jars, the faded colors, resembling ones that may have been there for a century.

Toward the end of the aisle on the left was the cereal section, and to the right were the crackers and cookies. The canned goods sat untouched for the most part, but the boxed and wrapped items had been strewn about, ripped apart, and somewhat consumed.

The sun had begun to set, and I turned to take the can of peas from the shelf. It was then that I froze in terror. His growl said it all. At the other end of the aisle was a large male black bear. We stood and stared at each other for what was a brief moment, yet it seemed like an eternity for me.

I was scared to death, but looked him in the eye and said, "Hey, I just want a can of peas."

Our eyes were connected in an apparent stare down. I slowly reached up, took a can off the shelf, and began backing away. He tilted his head in a way that made me feel less threatened.

Many thoughts raced through my mind, "His habitat is gone. He must be living in here. What if there are cubs?"

I turned and jumped over the barricades, dropping the can as I ran as fast as I could out of the store, leaving my new friend to his current domicile.

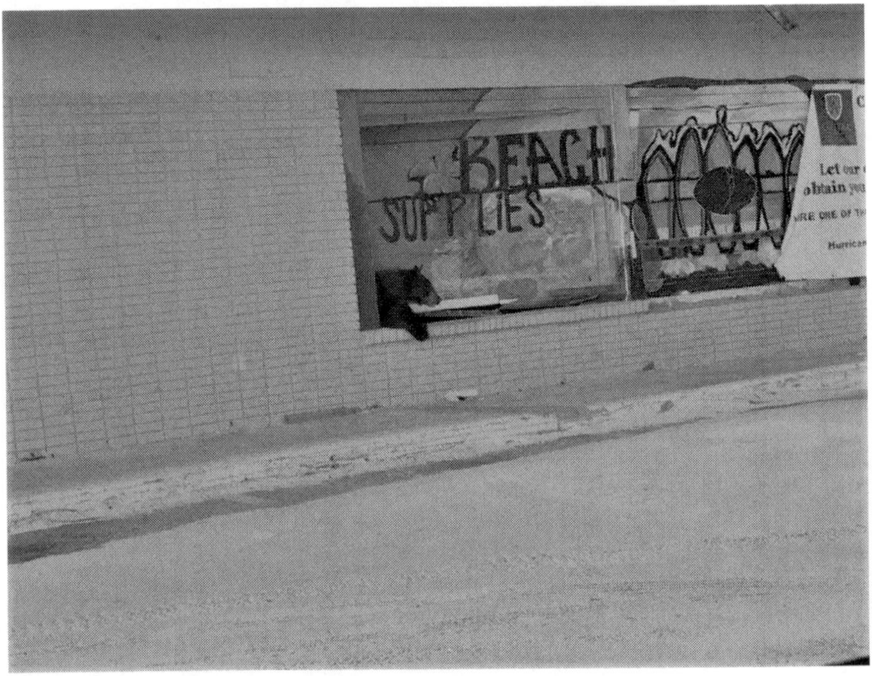
BEACH
SUPPLIES
Let our
obtain you

THE VERSATILITY OF VIEWPOINT

Through the course of these narratives, I realized how wonderfully therapeutic it was for me to write. My worries would subside, as I found myself at the keyboard for hours on end, jotting down my experiences and reflections in the aftermath of Hurricane Michael. I discovered a joy in writing; I could let my imagination go anywhere I wanted it to.

A few days after my encounter with the bear, I sat at my computer, pondering what it would be like to be one of the creatures that lived through the storm; to tell the story from a completely different point of view. I pictured two squirrels running for shelter.

That's when it happened.

Without thinking, I pressed the shift and quotation mark keys, followed by a line of text. I stopped abruptly, looking back at what I had just typed. An excitement shot through me.

The animals could talk! I felt a tidal wave of creativity come over me; the doors of possibility opening wide, my imagination knowing no boundaries.

THE FORGOTTEN FOREST: CAPTAIN'S CHRONICLES

It was mid-autumn, and the days had become cooler. A sense of freshness was in the air, and the forest was coming alive in anticipation of the new day. The adult squirrel arose from its nest, perching itself onto the strongest of limbs. It would seem a normal morning for most any creature of the wood, but this morning was different to this particular squirrel. He sensed something bad was coming, something out on the horizon, something deadly. He began looking around below, as if to be scouring the ground for acorns and such, when he focused on a broken, dried out tree limb.

His focus remained, as he scurried down the tree trunk. Once on the ground, he paused, remaining completely still. After two quick glances to the left and right, he jalumped over to a pile of fallen branches. He stood up erect, placed his hands behind his back, and began strolling by the wooden prospects like a drill sergeant.

"Too skinny,' he thought, then onto the next.

"Improper shape," he surmised.

The next fallen limb was judged, "incorrect vertex." The adult squirrel addressed the next specimen.

"Oh my, this one is perfect," he thought.

The squirrel was unaware that he was being watched. Out of the underbrush, two eyes were focused on him and his actions. The squirrel then attempted to procure his limb of choice by breaking it off from its host wood. The witness from the brush watched a few unsuccessful attempts, and then emerged from the foliage.

"Allow me to be of assistance!" stated the raccoon. The squirrel stood back; as the unexpected visitor broke the tree limb off, and laid it on the ground in front of him.

Without hesitation, the squirrel began gnawing on the limb. The bark was skillfully removed, as his sharp, precision teeth carved the wood. Just like a lathe, the natural artisan fashioned the blade, the hilt, the guards, and the pommel. He picked up his newly crafted sword, and instantly pointed it straight at the limb breaker.

The raccoon tilted his head in perplexity.

"My name is Loki, I am the captain of the sentries." stated the squirrel.

The bearer of the blade then demanded, "Who are you? What is your business here?"

The raccoon looked around, and spotted another, yet larger limb among the others. In short order, the lesser of the aggressors removed his limb of choice, and laid it down in front of the squirrel.

It appeared to both that there was a standoff, as the captain's sword continued to make a strong statement of defense. The raccoon broke the silence.

"Well enough, Captain," he stated, "My name is Rokai, leader of the sire's guard, and seasoned explorer among the humans. I wish for you to craft another sword, for myself."

"Why should I trust you?" inquired the well-armed defendant. The tip of the wood blade veered slightly off target.

The raccoon took advantage of the distraction, stating, "If not for me, you would still be tugging on that branch over there."

Sometimes, even in the natural world, logic can take effect, as it did that day. The squirrel drew back his weapon, placing it behind him.

"Let me see your hands," said the squirrel.

Rokai responded, "Again, I assure you that I mean no harm."

The Captain quickly replied, "I do not mean that! I must measure them for a proper fit. Now try to pay attention!"

PHOTO SHOOT

    I learned today, to never doubt your imagination; if you believe in something, go for it, if you dream it, it can come true. My newfound wild imagination led me to a toy store, where I bought some plastic animals, so I might study them in order to illustrate this book. I acquired a digital camera, and went out in the back yard, where I found a fallen tree limb and propped it up with an oak knot. I then picked up assorted branches here and there, creating a small scene. The next thing I know, I am flat on the ground with my face in the grass, looking up from different angles, taking photos.

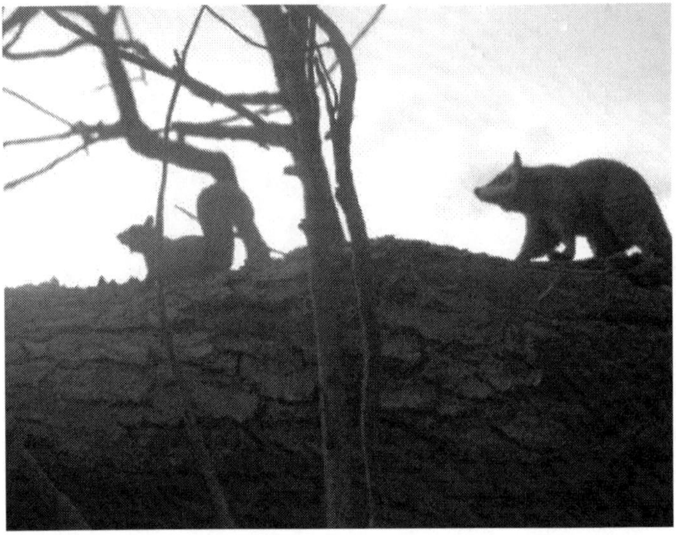

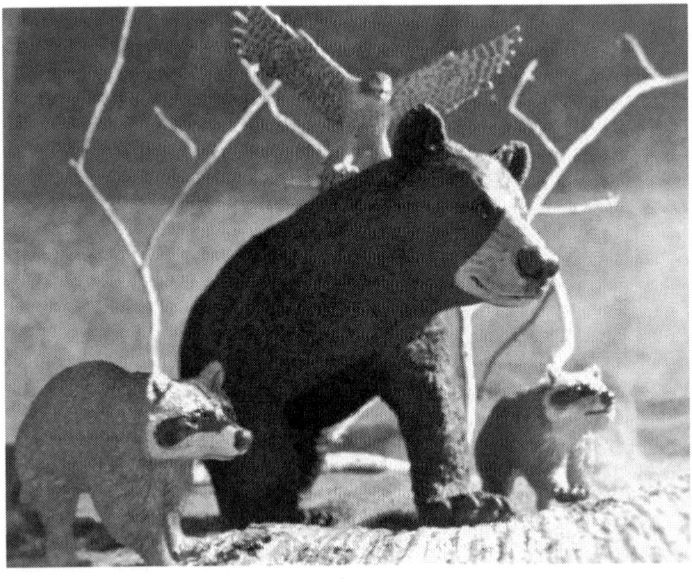

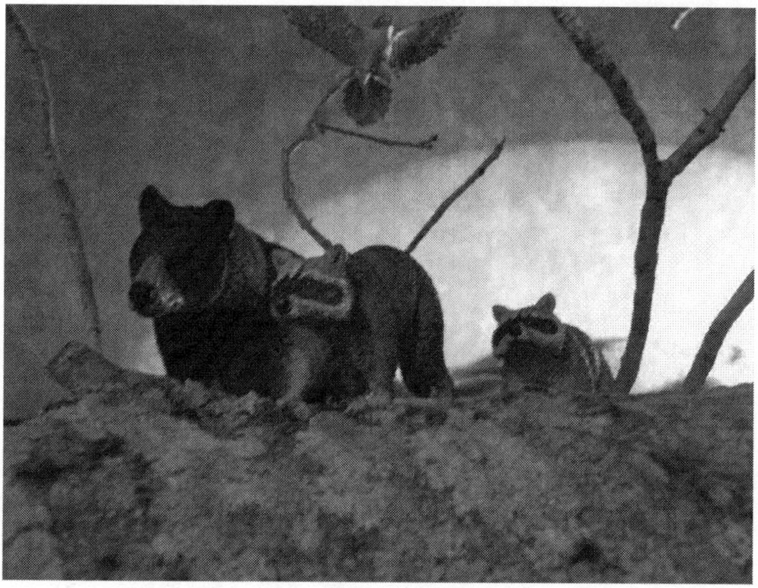

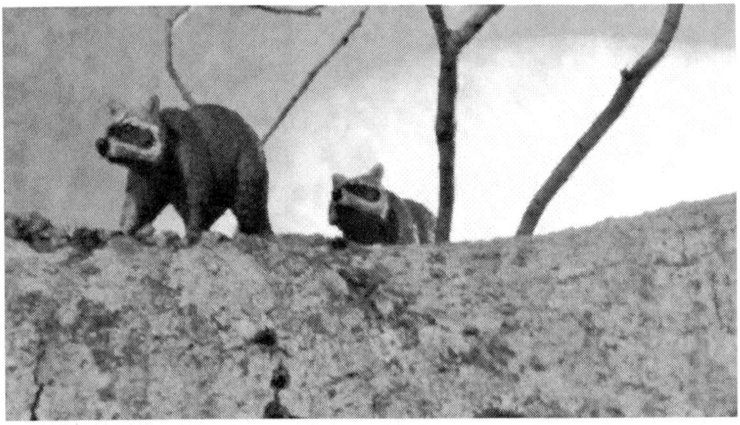

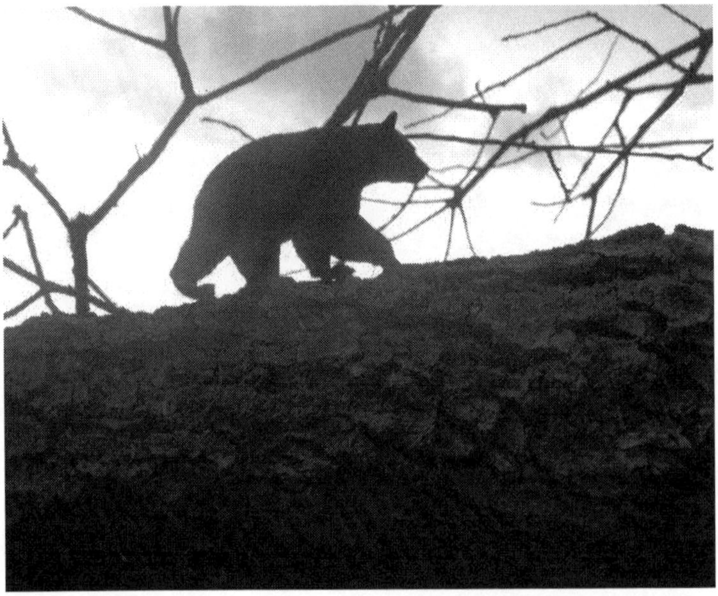

THE FORGOTTEN FOREST;
THE STORY OF THE GULF FOODS BEAR

On October 10, 2018, Hurricane Michael made landfall as a category 5 storm, and all but destroyed the small town of Mexico Beach, Florida.

In the center of the town lay a large wooded area. This is the story of the fourteen-acre forest as seen through the eyes of the creatures of the wood, and how they and the forest survived the storm, only to see it succumb to the destructive forces of the humans that surrounded it.

They lived in the large wood.
    They had no warnings.
    They had no way out....

    The trees began to sway profusely, and the squirrel sentries scurried toward the main burrow.
    "We must speak to Motok!" they exclaimed, "The winds are strong, and the seas are rising!"

Motok was the leader of the forest, a big clumsy oaf of a black bear.

In the center of the forest was the main burrow, the meeting place for the community of the forest. The trees were breaking over by then, and scared residents began running toward the burrow for shelter.

As the earth shook, the refugees came into the safe haven of the burrow. The birds flew off to the North-East; for they could not survive the strong winds that were quickly approaching. They rode away on large crests of currents ahead of the storm, as the squirrels evacuated their offspring from their nests high in the trees, securing a place inside the burrow. The raccoons were next in line, then the armadillo family. The winds became stronger. Inside the burrow was Motok, his queen, the two cubs, Mokie and Toomar, the squirrel family, a dozen or so of the raccoon clan, a number of armadillos, and a few assorted rodent refugees.

After the storm passed, the earth moving machines of the humans began to rumble the ground, and the sentries were aware. The team consisted of two raccoons, two squirrels, and a trusted hawk that had stayed behind. They went on scouting patrol, and once they had returned to the burrow, they reported to Motok.

Rokai was the leader of the sentries; a seasoned explorer among the humans; a crafty, stealthy raccoon of many years.   "What did you see?" Motok inquired.

"Sire, the humans burrows are all but destroyed as well," Rokai replied.

"I see," said the bear, "What were they speaking of?"

The raccoon gently bowed his head, then began glancing around the room, making eye contact with the elders and the others.

He looked back at Motok with a sarcastic grin and said, "It seems their largest fear is that they have no electricity, my Lord!"

The burrow erupted with hearty laughter, offering a few moments of pleasant distraction from their plight. Then the two squirrel sentries rushed in.

"The humans are destroying the forest!" they exclaimed.

In an instant, a large steel bucket on an excavator crushed through the burrow, and began ripping the century old trees from their roots.

"Quickly, to the sleeping chambers!" Motok shouted. The huge iron bucket raised towards the sky, then plunged again to the earth in a thunderous report, ripping tree after tree from its roots. Motok turned back in defiance, stood up, and let out a loud roar, and just as abruptly as it began, the destruction ceased; the machine lay still.

The humans retreated as the sun began to set. Motok told his queen, "We must seek shelter in the dwelling of the humans. The food is abundant there, and there is little time."

She responded, "But what of the others? They will surely perish."

Motok turned to his eldest son, Toomar, and spoke.

"My son, you must lead the others away from here. Follow the still water to the creek, then travel to the bend of the large river. To the north there is a new world, a wood the size of which you have never seen. Go there. I will stay behind until all have left."

"Send the sentries out to tell all creatures to prepare to flee." decreed Toomar. The sentries departed the burrow, and began their mission, venturing out into the jumbled chaos that was once a thriving forest.

The winds had blown a mailbox across the highway, and deposited it deep into the wood. Inside was a makeshift bed of thatched straw. The sentries approached.

"You there!" shouted Rokai, "You must leave with us on the eve. There is danger here."

A muffled voice came out from the rear. "I am Feezer, patriarch and leader of the Opossums. Go away!"

"The machines are near, you will surely perish if you stay," they sternly informed him.

He emerged from the mailbox, and slowly turned his head toward them, his aged, glazed eyes following after.

"Go, if you must," he muttered. "But I am too old and far too weary to make that journey. If this is to be my destiny, then so be it. Now scurry off, I must rest now." He turned back into his new found lair, and curled up onto the bed of straw.

The sentries looked at each other in disbelief, conferring with each other as to what to do.

The lead squirrel insisted, "There are many more creatures to warn, and very little time. We must keep moving."

The raccoon replied, "But we can't just leave the old geezer behind."

A muffled voice came from inside the mailbox.

"The name is Feezer!" exclaimed the opossum.

The team of sentries continued on their journey through the wood, working their way through the tangled trees and debris. Above, the hawk circled over, occasionally landing on a limb just ahead of the patrol on the ground. The raccoons, Rokai and Apollo, followed the two squirrels, Captain and Orion, who led the way deeper into the forest.

They soon came to an impasse; a large section of a human's burrow that had landed in the wood, completely blocking their familiar path. To the left was a long fence line that was the border into the land of the humans, and to the right of the obstacle was the wetland swamp, known to all creatures in the forest as the land of the legless lizards, or "snakes" according to the humans. The creatures of the wood knew well to never venture into the swamp, and there were many stories of animals venturing in, only to never be seen or heard from again. Legends told of a monster that lurked just below the surface of the water; virtually unseen by the naked eye, with huge jaws full of razor sharp teeth that could swallow a forest creature in one bite.

A tall tree had fallen from the force of the storm, breaking over at its base, creating a log bridge of sorts to the other side of the swamp. The four sentries stood at the water's edge, each one waiting for one of the others to say something.

It seemed like an eternity until Rokai broke the silence.

"Whatever our choice, we must all agree," he stated.

The youngest squirrel, Orion, was quick to chatter, "We should go back, we should really go back, and don't you think we should go back?"

The other three glanced at him for a perplexed moment, then focused back on the tree bridge. Apollo spoke up.

"We could climb over the fence into the land of the humans, and go around," he said confidently. Rokai turned to the eldest squirrel.

"What do you think, Captain?" he asked.

Captain responded, "Sir, if you are spotted by the humans or one of their dogs, it could mean certain death for you both."

Apollo raised his eyebrow as if he hadn't thought about that, and instantly agreed with the squirrel. Rokai interjected his opinion.

"If we go back, it could mean certain death for the creatures on the other side as well. I say we go forward."

The four looked at each other and nodded in agreement. The hawk had descended from his circular flight and had perched himself on the large roof section that was blocking the safe path. The team of sentries climbed the base of the fallen pine and began the journey to the other side of the swamp.

"Just look straight ahead, and don't lose your balance," Rokai instructed the others.

A number of legless lizards were perched in the branches on each side of them, watching their every move.

"We're halfway there," said Rokai, "Keep going…"

Just then a piece of bark slipped out from under Apollo's feet, tumbling him off the tree bridge and into the black water of the swamp. As the young raccoon struggled to stay afloat, two eyes broke the surface. The waters swelled as the large alligator turned, and began navigating straight toward the helpless raccoon. The remaining sentries raced to the other side, looking back in horror. The legend proved true, as the predator opened his huge jaws in anticipation for the kill. The frightened raccoon stopped struggling, and closed his eyes, ready to accept his fate. All at once a large shadow was cast over them, and seemingly out of nowhere, the hawk came plunging vertically through the trees, plucking the helpless victim from the water in its talons, then safely depositing him on the other side.

Rokai jumped in jubilation, and exclaimed, "Good job Hawkins! Bravo! Jolly good show!"

Apollo lay on the bank, wet and barely breathing, while the hawk stood vigilantly over him.

"I told you we should go back. We should have gone back," said the young squirrel.

They continued on their mission, canvassing the forest to inform the others. The top of the tree bridge continued into the wood, its branches and foliage creating a dense shrubbery.

They reconvened onto the path, as the hawk looked on from his perch above.

"Let's move along, lads!" Rokai suggested.

The sentries traveled along for the path until Rokai exclaimed, "Stillness and silence!"

Each member of the team froze in place instantly. A moment or two passed.

"I heard a rustling" said Rokai. The team remained still. The rustling noise occurred again, and the sentries turned to focus on its source.

"Under there," spoke Apollo, as he peered into the dense shrubbery. A further rustling, then they saw it. The most beautiful snow white feathers they had ever seen.

"Quickly! We must save her!" shouted Rokai.

Each one of the team began feverishly assisting each other in removing the layers of debris and foliage. Once revealed, the sentries looked in awe.

"Oh, my creator!" gasped Apollo softly, as he peered into her blue eyes.

The large white crane had been struck by flying debris as she attempted to escape with the other large birds. Caught in the tail winds, she lost lift, and landed into the wood. She began to rise, standing up on her thin, shaky legs, until she stood erect.

The sentries were all looking up at her, as she towered above them. Her wing feathers were ruffled and intertwined in total disarray. Apollo was enamored.

"What is your name?" he asked.

The young squirrel, Orion, rolled his eyes as he looked toward Apollo and chattered, "Stop being silly. We all know that birds can't talk!"

The slightly offended raccoon responded, "How are you sure? Maybe she simply hasn't had anything to say until now."

As the squirrel began his rebuttal, Rokai intervened.

"Stop this foolishness!" he ordered, "She must take flight immediately!"

Suddenly, the majestic bird began to outstretch its wings, and continued until they were as wide as she was tall. She began shaking her head almost violently, then flapping her wings back and forth with the same intensity, until each and every feather had realigned and layered itself perfectly back into place.

"Sir, the bird cannot gain lift from here, her wings will surely strike the branches." reported Captain.

"Then we shall lead her down the path that follows the sun," instructed Rokai, "There she can return to the sky."

The sentry team returned to the path, the crane following cautiously behind. The unlikely caravan arrived at the end of the path that follows the sun, where there was an opening in the fence.

The sentries led the large crane into the clearing just beyond the border into the land of the humans. The sun was beginning to set. She began flapping her wings, quickly gaining lift. The sentry team watched, as the majestic bird gently flew away toward the horizon.

"G-Goodbye Miss Lilly", mumbled Apollo…

The skies were becoming dark, and it was time for the sentries to begin the evacuation of the forest. They arrived at the last remaining thicket where the creatures of the forest had assembled. Then they rested.

It was the darkest of nights, there was no moon to be seen.
"It's time," said Toomar, "Follow me, I will lead you."

One by one, the creatures of the wood began their exodus through the land of the humans, in hopes of finding the new wood, their new world.

The stars began to fade, and the creatures knew what that meant. The sky became softer blue; the new day was coming, and so were the humans..

Soon it would be dawn, when the humans would continue their mission of destruction. The machines came back to life, continuing to claw their way through the Fourteen Acre Wood, leaving nothing in their path.

Motok had since migrated into the all but destroyed grocery store, from where he had witnessed the loads of debris being piled high in the trucks, carrying away all that was the forest with them. He squinted through a large crack in the wall, focusing on one of the trucks. He could see the crushed remnants of the mailbox in the mix of the refuse as it pulled away.

"Surely that stubborn old opossum could not have survived that crushed mailbox," he softly spoke out loud. He wondered how many other creatures of the forest had succumbed to the humans machines.

He was suddenly startled to hear a voice behind him say, "Yes, my Lord, good thing I wasn't in it at the time."

He turned around to see none other than Feezer himself, peeking out from behind a display case.

"Come out of the shadows, Geezer, for you are safe here," Motok said. The meek marsupial slowly and reluctantly came out and stood before the huge black bear.

"The name is Feezer, my Lord," he said as his voice trembled in fear.

"Is there anything I can do for you?" Motok asked.

"Maybe one thing, Sire," said the opossum sheepishly. He then turned and hobbled over toward one of the shelves. He reached up, displaced one of the dusty cans, and watched it fall to the floor. He then took his snout and began rolling the can down the center aisle, navigating through the trash and debris, until it came to a rest at Motok's feet. The old 'possum sat back on his two hind legs, and glanced up with an expression of despair, hunger, and trust.

The large bear turned toward the tiny creature, picked up the can, and ripped the top off with his massive jaws. He then poured the salty boiled peanuts out on the floor in front of him.

"Eat well, my friend," said the bear. "Now we must sleep, for as soon as the sun leaves the sky, we shall embark on our journey to the new wood, and reconvene with the others."

Motok turned and began trudging down the center aisle toward the rear of the store, turning past the shelving into the open stockroom. He lay down gently next to his queen and their youngest cub, Mokie.

The afternoon had passed, and darkness was beginning to consume the sky. The queen arose from her slumber, and walked down the center aisle, with young Mokie close behind.

She arrived at the piled up display cases and coolers that had formed a barricade from the open part of the building. Seeing an opening, she decided to go through it in search of food.

Suddenly, a large steel gate crashed down behind her, trapping the female bear.

The startled cub lurched back, and as the humans rolled the trap out and into the center of the open store, Motok awoke from the noise. Two humans entered through the opening, with beams of light shining on the frightened young bear.

"There is a cub!" one human exclaimed, as it turned and ran toward the center aisle.

The humans quickly pursued the tiny escapee, their lights flailing around, trying to keep the beams focused on him. From behind a partition, Motok instantly emerged, and stood before the approaching perpetrators. Mokie ran quickly between his father's legs, as the great bear flexed his arms and let out a loud roar. The panicked humans drew their weapons.

One of them screamed, "My God, I thought there was only one!" And in a fraction of a second, the device of the humans discharged, its projectile striking the large black bear directly in the chest. The mighty Motok collapsed to the floor, and was still.

The cub was paralyzed with fear, as it looked up at the approaching humans. One of them extended a pole of sorts, and Mokie felt a rope tighten around his neck. The humans pulled the struggling cub closer, then placed him into a small cage of his own.

Through an opening in side of the trap, the helpless queen witnessed them place her captured cub in the back of a truck. She then saw a large number of humans who were picking up Motok's body, and dragging it into the back of another vehicle.

"We had better hurry before this tranquilizer dart wears off!" she heard one say.

The two vehicles pulled out of the parking lot, and began driving toward the outskirts of town. The convoy went over a small bridge, and the female bear watched through the grates of her rolling prison cell. The lights from the town became smaller, and smaller, eventually disappearing from her view, as it continued to travel away from the land of the humans.

"It's right up here, Frank," one of the officers informed the other, "to the right."

The trucks turned onto a dirt road, and continued their journey deeper into the wood.

"Slow down, it's hard to find," said one.

"There it is," replied the other. The two vehicles turned down a narrow, rocky path. As the trucks bounced back and forth, Motok began to awake from his drug induced slumber. They came to a stop near the water's edge and Motok sat up, somewhat groggy. He witnessed the humans opening the grate.

"Time to go, Precious!" said one of the officers, as he slapped the side of the trap. The other human had placed the cage containing Mokie a short distance away, and released the door. The female bear jumped out and ran to meet her cub, while Motok rolled out of the back of the truck. The trio reconvened, and quickly disappeared into the wood.

"Hey Frank!" exclaimed one human, "Looks like we got us a stowaway!" Out from under a tarp emerged none other than Feezer himself. The officers helped escort him from the bed of the pick-up.

"Go on, little fellah," one said, as they watched the elder opossum retreat into the darkness.

Morning came, and Motok stood at the edge of the still water, the trees on the banks forming a canopy of foliage overhead.

"We must go this way," he told the others, making a gesture toward the North. As the three began their migration, Motok looked back, to see the old opossum sitting still.

"Come along, now, we must be going," he informed the marsupial.

"Sire, I regret that you must continue without me, for I am too old and far too weary to make the journey," was the reply.

"Nonsense!" stated the bear, as he turned around. The mighty Motok picked up the frail opossum, and placed him upon his back. The entourage traveled along the edge of the still water, until they approached a clearing in the canopy.

"There it is!" exclaimed the bear.

The bend of the large river lay just ahead. The travelers quickened their pace, for they knew they had arrived at their new home. They heard a loud screeching sound from above, and paused to look up. A large formation flew overhead, led by the trusted sentry Hawkins, followed by Lilly the white crane and the other birds of the Fourteen Acre Wood. The great Hawk screeched again, signaling the arrival of the leader of the forest to all the other creatures that had fled the land of the humans.

Toomar and the sentries emerged from the forest, followed by the others, as the birds settled into the treetops of their new home.

"Welcome home, Sire," said Rokai.

It was then, that the forest echoed with laughter.

THE DAY OF THE PELICAN

The mullet boat created few waves, as the two fishermen trolled along the shoreline. With the rising sun against their backs, they ventured out from the familiar slough, the crisp, cool breeze welcoming them into the deeper waters of the gulf. Hopes were high of netting fish between the beach and the sand bar, as the pelicans flew in from the south on their daily routine in search of food.

Every morning the birds would canvass the shallow waters of the bay, seeking out schools of fish. Once on target, they would dive in headfirst, scooping up their prey that lay just below the surface. Mothers would dive as well, but not for themselves. The gatherers would store them in their lower beaks, and then head back home to feed their hatchlings. The elders would fly above the rest, allowing the youngers to feed first. Most would catch their fish for the day in short order and turn back, but others did not. The fishing boats of the humans had been steadily harvesting fish, and the pelicans could tell the numbers were dwindling.

The unlucky fishers would then glide into the Mexico Beach canal, perch upon a pier post, and feed on scraps tossed out by the fishermen. The dock posts became a frequent habitat for the elders of the colony.

After the storm, the humans rebuilt their own personal habitats, yet installed cones on top of every post, forbidding the elders from lighting on them. The colony was forced to reside on the ruins of a long lost pier, where food was scarce for the hungry birds. The mullet boat returned. As the small skiff meandered along the shore, the fishermen would lower their nets, successfully harvesting every pogie in its wake. The pelicans would follow close behind, yet there were no fish left for them.

The leadership gathered at sundown, each taking his perch on the secluded dock posts.

"The humans are taking all of the food!" One said.

"Agreed!" Spoke another.

The Grand Master informed them, "There are many fish for us, and the humans rarely take many with their little poles and hooks."

The Pelican crew chuckled among themselves.

"But they have nets now," said Octavius, "Two men need not all of the fish in the sea!"

"It's true!" spoke up another, "If the humans return on the morrow, we could all perish from starvation!"

Octavious turned to the Grand Master, and said, "My Lord, we must stop the two humans at all costs. I beg permission to intervene."

"So be it," spoke the eldest. "Lead a patrol to monitor the threat".

"With all respects, my Lord, we could be monitoring our own demise!" responded the colonel, as he looked around at the others. "We must eliminate the threat as well."

The assembly nodded in agreement, as the sun began to set. Throughout the night, the pelicans rested on their perches, while the stars rotated around them. The soft hues of daylight emerged from the east, signaling the beginning of a new day. The flock began to awaken, each one preparing to begin their daily flight along the coastline.

The boat with the big net was again on its course into the bay, and all pelican eyes were on it. The two men followed the shoreline past the wind marked beach, and into the channel towards the beach called Mexico.

The fishermen lowered their nets, as dozens of pelicans assembled in a V-shaped formation above. At the front of the squadron was the Grand Elder, with General Octavious on his left.

To the right, was the adventuresome Cyprio, accompanied by his son, Philo. Seagulls were following close to the vessel, while the fish began to get caught in the seine. The two humans slowed their troll, in preparation of reaping their catch of the day. They pulled in the nets, opened a large door in the bottom of the boat, and began spilling the bountiful harvest into the hold below.

One exclaimed, "Woo hoo!" "Check this out, Earl!"

He then untangled an infantile sea turtle from the net, and held it up like a trophy. The startled reptile began flapping its fins, in a desperate plea for freedom.

"Dammit Edwin!" the other human retorted, "I already told you these nets ain't legal! Don't go showin' off about it."

Then he added, "He will look good next to that big bass on my fireplace, though!" The two erupted in heartless laughter, while placing the turtle in the forward hold. Again the nets were lowered. The pelican patrol began a gradual turn, looping around in circular formation, reconvening behind the illegal fishers.

The nets continued to trap almost everything in its path. A few small pogies escaped, and quickly became the focus of the youngers.

The birds began to dive for the escapees. Loose fishes were flopping on the deck of the boat, enticing the other flyers to come closer in. The cargo hold was overflowing, yet the view from the sky reflected no fish in the sea for the hungry birds.

"I'm going in," declared Philo. The younger then dove sharply out of formation, descended in altitude, furled back his wings, and landed on the back of the boat.

"What is that?" shouted Earl, as he stood face to face with the majestic bird. Suddenly, the other human grabbed a gaff hook, and swung it toward the feathered hitch hiker, barely missing its beak.

The intended victim fell backward, landing on a portion of the net. His webbed foot became entangled, as he feverishly flapped his wings. His escape attempt proved futile, when suddenly, a handheld net swooped down from above, snaring the struggling bird.

"Looks like we've got us another trophy!" Earl bragged. His partner in crime then carried the hostage to the front of the skiff, laying the bound victim on top of the bin that held the imprisoned sea turtle.

"The holds are full. Let's head on in," suggested one. They both opened another beer, and turned sharp to port, maintaining a heading toward the familiar slough. The leaders of the flock were enraged. As they monitored from overhead, they began to confer with one another.

"We must rescue Philo" declared Cyprio.

"Agreed," responded Octavious, "Perhaps we can kill two humans with one stone. We shall attack the boat, forcing it to run aground."

The unsuspecting crew continued trolling past the wind marked beach, unaware that the flying formation was following so close behind. The feathered force grew larger, as other pelicans arrived to join the airborne armada.

The boat made its way around the bend, allowing the canal entrance to come into view. On the left of the waterway lay a boat ramp, a popular gathering place for the humans.

General Octavious announced, "My fellow pelicans, prepare to attack!"

Cyprio interjected, "Not yet, Lads! Just a little closer." He continued to advise, "Closer still…Closer," then he nodded to the General.

"Left flank, engage!" ordered the leader, "Right flank, engage!"

The formation separated, with the right flank maintaining altitude, while the left flank descended, skimming along the surface.

In regimented order, the two forces reconvened on the target, and one by one, the attackers pummeled the poachers. The humans on shore heard the screams, and watched as hundreds of pelicans converged on the tiny boat. The captain fell backward and landed on the engines throttle, while losing control of the helm. The wayward vessel shot toward the bank and ran aground, wedging the hull between two large boulders. The force of the impact sent the pile of nets forward, landing them on top of the poachers. The nets were heavy, and the more the men struggled to gain freedom, the more entangled they became.

The startled humans gathered around the scene, with two bystanders climbing their way into the wreck. One rescuer stated, "Just stop moving. We'll cut you out of there." The un-entanglement process was underway, when two police officers arrived.

"What happened here?" they inquired.

A young girl and her little brother were standing nearby.

"We saw it, Sir. The boat came in, and the pelicans attacked them," she said.

The boy spoke up excitedly, "Yeah! It was awesome! They were hitting those guys like out of a machine gun! They were like Kamikazes!"

The Officers boarded the vessel, thinking how odd of an

occurrence this was. "Why would they behave in this manner?" asked one.

The second officer glanced toward the bow, and said "Look over here. I bet this is why."

The two knelt down next to the captured pelican, and carefully began removing him from the bondage of the bungee cords. Once freed, the rescuers held him up, and sent him aloft. The young Philo quickly flapped his wings and gained flight, only to fly around in a tight circle, landing back on the bow in front of them.

"Go on now, little fella," one said, as they turned toward the stern. The young bird shook its wings and began grunting loudly, while thrusting and snapping its bill.

"What is it, Buddy?" inquired the officer.

"He wants to show us something," stated the other. Philo hopped down on the lid to the secret compartment, shaking his head erratically. The investigators opened the hold, discovering the sea turtle hidden inside. The two volunteers saw what was happening, and stopped trying to free the busted poachers.

The crowd around the boat had grown larger, as a Marine wildlife officer arrived.

The officer handed her the lethargic reptile, and she quickly turned toward the shore. She placed the stunned turtle into the shallow water, where it soon swam away into the bay. The agents stepped over the trapped men, opening the rear hold.

"Oh my goodness, Boys, you two are in a big heap of trouble," said one Officer. The galley was full of shads, croakers and pogies, which were the main food source for the pelican colonies; but there were other species as well, including juvenile red fish, trout fingerlings, baby groupers, and others.

"We need buckets of sea water," announced the rescuers.

A few spectators ran to their trucks, and then to the shore, while others joined in to form a brigade of sorts. Most of the creatures were still living, and time was of the essence.

The badged trio donned their gloves and culled through the fishy populace, placing them into the impromptu rescue containers. Bucket by bucket, the displaced fishes were returned to the sea. By this time, the squadron had regrouped, and was gliding above in triumph. There were still many bait fish remaining in the lower bin, as the pelican squadron flew in for a landing. The successful battalion lined up along the shore in ceremonial fashion and watched the officers continue to fill the buckets. One officer paused, looked up at the pelicans, and said to his partner, "You want to know what I'm thinking?"

"Probably the same thing I'm thinking," was the response.

"Yep," he nodded, "I'm thinking its suppertime."

THE MIRACLE

I was sitting at the car wash awaiting my turn when my cell phone began to ring. I answered, and for a moment the world stood still. The conversation that followed was an exchange of emotions, questions, and vague answers.

"I'm on my way," I exclaimed, as I placed the truck in drive and exited the car wash. I stopped to pick up a friend.

"I need you to follow me; there's been a bad accident."

We drove to my house where I got in my car, and began the trek towards Wewahitchka.

The events of the past six months began to circulate through my mind, intermingling with thoughts of what I had just heard. I've had many moments recently doubting God, wondering why did he let the storm happen, why did he take so much from me and so many others; why did he let the thieves steal what was left; why did he let the rats in to consume the few clothes I salvaged? Why, dear God, now this? I pulled up to the wrecker yard and the attendant let me in.

At first I did not recognize it, but then I saw it. The little car I bought my daughter the year prior on her 16th birthday was now a mangled wreck. The driver's door was crushed into the seat, and the dashboard was folded in towards the center. The windows were shattered. The front bumper was gone.

I turned to the wrecker driver, and said, "There's not enough room in there for her now, the airbag did not deploy. How could anyone survive this?"

"Only an act of God" he responded.

I left the yard and began driving toward Honey Ville, trying to hold back the wave of emotions; I needed to stay strong. I pulled into the gravel driveway, placed the car in park, and dialed the number.

"I'm out in the driveway," I said.

A moment later, the front door opened. She came down the steps, looked at me, and said, "Hey Daddy!"

My little girl was banged and bruised, and had large cuts on her arms and legs, many with stitches. I have felt many emotions in my life, but nothing can compare to the feeling of seeing your child injured. I tried not to let her see me crying.

"Make sure you check the oil baby, it has a small leak." I said, as I handed her the key.

"Where did it happen"? I asked, and she explained. It was right down the road on the highway, with steep ditches and trees not far off of the shoulder.

I pulled out of the driveway, and headed toward the crash site. The day was overcast and gloomy. Around the bend, I saw the skid marks. She had left the highway at almost 70 miles per hour, overcorrected and crossed the other lane, then spun toward the ditch, slamming into a tree. The force of the impact must have been immense.

Her surviving this was nothing short of a miracle in my eyes. I pulled the front bumper out of the ditch, and started walking toward the truck. My thoughts overwhelmed me, and I paused to look up toward the sky.

It was then that I realized that the same God that I had doubted earlier, the same God that I questioned, the same God that I had turned my back on, was the same God that saved my baby's life. The clouds had begun to disperse, as the sunbeams pierced their way through the openings in the overcast canopy...

It was then, that I wept...

SEPTEMBER 17, 1961

So, just how would one write an autobiography? A story of one's life, as told by the one who lived it; I suppose one should start at the very beginning. Yet in this regard, I don't remember much. Memories of my first years are merely glimpses into a subconscious recollection of images and events. It was "Astro boy" ...that's it. The first image I remember seeing as a child was a black and white cartoon, which was rare, because little did we see television then.

I remember living in California, I was 4, my brother Stephen, 5, and my sister Lisa, a mere 3 years old; Lisa was the apple of my eye. I went to kindergarten across the street, and from what I remember, it was a celebration of cookies, milk, and naps on a mat. In my mind, I can still feel my cheek stuck to the vinyl whilst I woke up slobbering.

There was a kid next door, he was a pest, and had warts under his nose like a mustache. One day, he was being mean to another child, and fell, busting his lip open. There was blood. Our Mommies came to the rescue, and we were rewarded with peanut butter and jelly sandwiches.

Daddy was in the Air Force, so halfway through the first grade, we had to move. Momma said we were going to live with Grandma in Birmingham, Alabama, where she was born and raised, because daddy had to go to a place called Vietnam.

I loved getting to Grandma's. It felt like home; she lived on a hill, Papaw burned coal in the fireplace, and we would be warm there. The bedrooms were so cold you better have had your pajamas on and get under the covers quick. She had a wood burning stove outside in a shanty, where she would put up her preserves. She also had muscadine grape vines running down the hill, and Papaw fetched them. I found out later in life that she made wine out of them.

Grandma had a big house that Papaw built on the side of the hill. We three young'uns arrived somewhere around 1966.

Momma got a job and tasked granny with taking us to school each mornin', and pickin' us back up afterwards. Some days, granny would tell us to walk home.

It was a small-town street, maybe a mile if that, but I have fond memories of my life walking home, in the first grade, like I was somebody. The first thing I passed was a small ravine, under a bridge, with a flow of water, and then we walked by the roller-skating rink. Halfway home was a little store, and I would stop there. I will never forget walking up into that store with my 25 cents. It had those screen doors with the springs on them that would slap back shut.

The door had a Sunbeam bread sign. I would get a honey bun and a little carton of chocolate milk and sit out on the curb.

I was, then, on top of the world.

Once we got to Grandma's, we had to climb the hill to get to the house. She had to drive up a steep gravel road, and the driveway was on top of the hill. I used to love the sound her car tires made as we drove up it. My Papaw's name was Hobert, and Grandma's was Bertha Mae, but everyone called her Berthie.

Daddy got to stay for Christmas before going to Vietnam. We didn't have much, but my brother and I had found two rusty bicycles and tried to ride them, but could not. Christmas morning, there were two shiny bicycles for me and brother. Mine was blue, and had rubber grips, with tassels hanging off of them. I was the king of the hill with my bicycle. Steven wrecked on his the first day, trying to jump a plywood ramp, and scratched some paint off. He said it wasn't a new bike. "Daddy painted our old ones." He never rode it again. I didn't care, I loved my bike, and I rode it everywhere.

One day Grandma let us two boys paint something. We each had a brush, and when we were done playing she told us to go wash them out. We went up the hill, and spotted Papaws bath tub by the shed. It was full of water and there were some big catfish living in it. Steven and I put the wet paint brushes in with the catfish. Later that afternoon Papaw came home and got mighty angry. His catfish were floating upside down.

There was a narrow, concrete walkway leading from the shed on top of the hill down to the house. The muscadine vines ran down the hill alongside.

One day while picking grapes, I encountered a hornet's nest. One of them went straight for my throat and stung me good. Papaw grabbed me, reached down between his cheek and gum, and pulled out his chewin' terbacky. Before I knew it, he smacked that wet terbacky on my neck.

"Stay still, boy! This 'll take the sting out!" I trusted Papaw and stopped trying to escape. The pain stopped almost instantly. Berthie Mae put me in the bathtub right away.

The leaves on the trees were big. One day they all started falling on the ground, and before long, we were running and playing through them on the top of the hill.

It was just getting dark, and Berthie hollered for us young 'uns to "Git in the house."

We three ran down the hill, tumbling and laughing all the way, through the leaves. I tumbled to a stop and felt something tingling in my hand. I looked at it, and it was so dark it seemed to be covered in black oil. But it was blood. I had landed on a broken glass coke bottle and cut myself real bad. Papaw grabbed me, rushed me to the sink, and put my hand under the water to get a good look at it. Then he said "Berthie, start the car." I think I knew what that meant. We loaded up in the car, and headed down the hill to go to the hospital.

Just past the school was a railroad crossing, and we had to stop for the train. We waited a long time, and Berthie kept saying that it was the longest train that there ever was. Momma had wrapped my hand in a towel, but it bled so bad the whole thing was red when we got there.

A doctor gave me stitches and wrapped up my little hand like a boxing glove. For the next day or so, I could have all of the peanut butter and jelly sandwiches I wanted.

It was 1967, and I was 6 years old.

I think Papaw had everything there was to have. On the side of the hill, behind the house were his coal and firewood bins, dug into the hill, and wrapped with old roofing tin. He had apple trees too. He would grow things called gourds and make birdhouses out of them. Birds loved Papaw; they were everywhere. One day he was digging in the garden.

"Whatcha doin' Papaw?" I asked.

"Why, I'm diggin' up taters," he said.

"Why are the taters in the ground, Papaw?" I asked.

He said, "I planted them. That's where they grow."

I thought they came from the store. I loved taters, so I started digging with him. We dug up that whole patch. I think I wound up in the bathtub over that, too.

There was always a warm fire going at Grandmas, and she was often cooking beans and cornbread. Sometimes she would bake apples. She had a clock that looked like a cat, and its tail would swing back and forth. We always knew what time it was.

One day I was reading one of Grandma Berthie's magazines. The ad said I could buy three books for ten cents. There was a circle on a card for you to tape a dime on it. I had a dime, and a stamp.

I sent it, without telling anyone, and I was mailed three books right away: <u>Daniel Boone</u>, <u>Robinson Caruso</u>, and <u>Tom Sawyer.</u> Then three more books came, with a bill for ten dollars, then three more, with another bill. Momma said we had to send them back.

In the living room was a fireplace, and on the mantle was a photo of a young man in a uniform. Grandma told me he was my Uncle Kenneth, and that he was killed in the war. He was Papaw and Berthie's first born child, and Momma's brother. There was a flag folded in a triangle next to it. It stayed cold in there because she kept the door shut. We all stayed by the fireplace near the kitchen. Later in life I researched the National Archives Military death records, and found him on the registry. It read:

"White, Hobart Jr, Private first class, United States Marine Corps. Mother, Mrs. Bertha M. White, Route 7, Box 115b, North Birmingham"

He must have been killed around 1944. To this day, whenever I look at photographs from that era, the landing on D-Day, the march toward Berlin, the liberation of the death camps, I find myself looking at the faces of the marines in the photos, trying to find his image in one of them.

Across the street on Lewisburg Road lived an elderly lady. We would see her sweep her porch, and sometimes she would bring us cookies. She could not climb the hill, so us kids would run down to get them. Grandma Berthie called her "Two Mamas" because of being a Great Grandmother. They were good friends, Berthie and Two Mamas.

The year had passed, and Daddy got to leave Vietnam. Momma and us three young 'uns went to a place called "Japan" to be with him. He was in the Air force. We had to stay there for five years.

THE JAPAN DIARIES

It was a long flight on a big airplane to get to Japan. The air force base was surrounded by a tall wire fence, and you had to go to the gate to get in. At the gate there were men with guns, but if you waved at them, they would let you go in. Daddy had already got us a little house to live in, but it was outside of the fence.

Across the street was a young Japanese family. The walls of their house were made of bamboo frames and rice paper. I got to visit them often. They had a table that was so low to the floor, you had to sit on your ankles on a pillow to eat dinner with them. The aromas from her kitchen were different than anything I had ever smelled, but were amazing.

She would say "konichiwa", which means hello in Japanese.

Their bathroom was a big hole in the ground in the backyard, surrounded by bamboo.

I quickly started school on base. We lived outside of the high fence; it had barbed wire on top of it. Sometimes at night we would hear chanting and shouting. The Japanese demonstrators would burn torches, while holding banners saying "Yankee, go home." Mama said to not pay them any attention, that we wasn't Yankees, we was Southerners.

The first day of school we stood out in the snow, and waited for the school bus. Soon it arrived and we got on it. There was a Japanese man driving the bus. He seemed nice, and wore a uniform with white gloves. I got off of the bus, only to get back on it to go home for lunch. Then, back on the bus to go back to school. When we stopped, all of the kids got off of the bus except me.

As I did not recognize my surroundings, I approached him and said, "This is not my school." He spoke in Japanese and forced me to exit the bus.

It was at that moment I was lost, and I walked away in the wrong direction.

The rain began to drizzle, and I sought shelter under a small tree. All of the buildings looked the same, and I kept walking toward the wrong gate of the military base, thinking I was almost home. The guards let me walk by unnoticed.

Darkness fell, and the rain turned cold. I turned down a street, where there were Japanese vendors, colorful lights, torches, noise, and squid on a stick. An old lady confronted me in a language I did not understand. When I responded, she began slapping me in the face profusely, while holding on to my collar. I wrestled away, and ran down the street, as she kept shouting.

It was freezing cold and dark by then, and I sat down on a bench. I pulled my jacket up over my face, tucking my hands in my pockets.

A short while later, A Japanese police officer came up to me, and gestured toward an office down the street. I followed him into a small room, where there was a heater. I was scared, cold, and lost. An hour or so went by, and the shivering subsided.

Suddenly, an air force policeman from the base pulled up to get me. I got to ride back across the base in his patrol car. It was late, and Mama was crying.

I started the third grade, and that's where I learned how to write. We had these jumbo pencils. There were dotted lines on the paper, and you had better stay inside of them. On the first day, I proudly picked up my jumbo pencil, and started writing my first letters ever. I found myself immersed in it, and continued until my hand began to hurt a little. I simply placed the pencil in my other hand, and kept drawing letters and numbers.

Suddenly I heard a shout. "No!" exclaimed the teacher, as she took out a ruler, and smacked me real hard on my left hand.

It hurt real bad, so I looked up at her and asked, "Why did you do that?"

She said, "Don't argue with me!" while snatching the pencil out of my left hand, placing in my right. I continued to write the letters again, feeling somewhat crushed emotionally. As I scrolled along, I realized I felt more comfortable with my left hand, so I placed the pencil back into it. Instantly, I was a writer! I could make big letters, and small ones too! I started drawing a mouse out of an "a".

The disgruntled instructor stood up from her desk, and came

towards me. "Come outside with me!" she screamed. I was snatched up by the collar and violently escorted out of the classroom, and into the hallway.

What happened next is somewhat blurry, except for the memories of the teacher pointing, screaming and slapping me in the face over and over, so hard that my glasses flew off onto the floor.

"Don't come back in my classroom until you have stopped crying," she said, as she went back inside. I walked down the empty hallway toward the water fountain, drank some water, and then washed my face. At that moment, something changed. Something happened inside that little boy. I was so young, so innocent; I knew nothing, but I thought to myself then that maybe I was alone in this world, that maybe no one would ever understand me. I felt different from the others.

I went home and said nothing of it. The next day, I put my pencil in my left hand again, and received another beating in the hallway, but the second one was worse. The next morning I told my mother that I did not want to go to school, and explained why. The next thing I know, me and momma are at the school, with the teacher and some really important looking man.

I had to face my abuser, while telling the man what happened.

The next day, we had a new teacher. She was real nice, and she let me write with any hand I wanted. I realized then that I was ambidextrous.

It was 1969, I was 8 years old.

The next year after school, I had to take Judo lessons. I was told it was the art of self-defense. It did not make much sense to me at first, but I must have thought to myself, "Why not?" I was in Japan less than a week, and had been beaten up twice by two different women."

So, off we went. Me and brother would walk to the meeting place, put on our judo outfits, and learn different postures and stances.

We would poise on the mat, then repeat precise movements, over and over, while swearing in Japanese.

The only memory I have of the instructor was when he told me, "Your strength lies in your defense."

He would also say, "Never let the opponent see your weakness."

He would tell me that every time we went to Judo lessons.

One maneuver was how to protect yourself when falling. We would lunge forward towards the mat, and curl our heads down with our shoulders following. We would then land on the mat in a rolling motion, ultimately hopping back up on our feet. Another maneuver was how to hold an opponent down, in such a way that he could not get up.

One day after school, as I was walking home, four boys intercepted me near the playground. One of them pushed me down, and the others began kicking and punching me while I laid on my back struggling to get up. A few days later, the gang targeted me again, but instead of fighting back, I just stood there.

"Go ahead," I said, "There's four of you, beat me up if you want to."

They looked perplexed and confused. One of the gang members said, "Let's get out of here."

As they turned to leave, so did I. The instigator of the violence grew angry and came running toward me with a full body tackle. I was never a fighter; I knew not how, but as we fell to the ground, that little boy on the judo mat emerged, and I used my leverage against him. I wound up on top of him in the judo hold.

He could not move. After he begged me to turn him loose, I conceded. Those boys never bothered me again...

Little did I know that years later in my life, the lessons would instinctively emerge from time to time.

In 2008, I was on a job site demolishing an old, existing building. The excavator had ripped the structure apart, and the debris lay about around the perimeter, with large nails protruding upwards, in amongst shards of splintered lumber. As I was monitoring the destruction, I glimpsed a movement of sorts underneath the pile. I raised my arms up to the operator.

"Stop, Chris!" I shouted, "There's something under there."

He turned off the machine, and I proceeded to get a foothold onto the boards. I tight-roped my way to the point of observation, pulling up a large piece of debris. Trapped underneath were two black kittens, one with white socks, one without. I retrieved them, passed them to a worker, and regained my balance. The bucket on the excavator shifted, and I instantly lost my footing. As I began to fall, I looked around behind me to the closest clearing.

It was about three feet away, and to save myself from impalement, I instinctively dove out of the debris pile. In a split second, that little boy on the judo mat instinctively returned, as I tucked my head, turned my shoulder downward, and rolled onto the grass, springing back up onto my feet afterward. As I turned around, my buddy shouted, "Nice tuck and roll, Dude!!" The other worker was looking at me dumbfounded. I felt like I had a super power, just like in the comic books I read back then.

Soon after, we moved on to the base at Yakota. Mama was real pretty, so daddy made her be a go-go dancer at the Officers club. He took pictures, and she was in the paper. Then she was a waitress there, working nights. Sometimes on Saturday night there was a show, and us three children got to go see it, and order a cheeseburger. We would sit at the large tables, order up a 'Shirley Temple" and feel like we were somebody.

It was 1972, and I was 11 years old.

I started school again and continued to be somewhat of a loner. I had a few friends, but most often my teachers would assign me special tasks, above what the other children were doing. I was in wonderment of the aquarium in the classroom and was tasked with taking care of it. I would remove the creatures from the soiled water, place them in a fresh refuge, and then clean the entire tank, while the other children were coloring or whatnot.

I became known for my talents, and for the next four years, each new teacher I had would place me in charge of their aquatic ecosystems. Some learned that I could draw and paint things, so I began painting and drawing images on the schools bulletin boards and creating backdrops for the school plays.

One thing we three children thought we missed the most was television. As there were no stations broadcasting in English at that time, there seemed no need to have one. Instead, we had our little FM radios, and every night at bedtime, we would all climb in the same bed, turn out the lights and tune into the far East network station, which would broadcast four thirty minute radio shows. The first one was "Dragnet", then "Fibber McGee and Molly," "The Great Gildersleeve,"and lastly "Playhouse 99".

The experience must have sharpened our imaginations, for as we lay in the darkness, the mental images we perceived were of our own creation. Every now and then, after we listened to a segment, I would ask my brother and sister a question about what we just heard. For example, in the soundtrack, a car might drive up, and we would hear the sound of the door opening and closing. I would ask them, "What color was that car?" in our minds, we each might perceive the car differently, and it was fun to compare what we each thought.

In a world without television, there was a lot of time to do other things, and I spent a lot of time creating things and reading. Momma had bought a set of encyclopedias, and I found that I would get immersed in them, going from topic to topic, sometimes reading for hours on end.

I was an average student and tended to spend more time drawing cartoons in class than listening to the teacher, but all those hours reading mommas encyclopedias must have made a positive impression on me, because I scored highly on an aptitude test given to students at my school. So high, in fact, that a teacher went to my parents and asked them if I could attend an experimental class that taught something called "Phonics". I firmly believe that between the knowledge I gained in that class, coupled with what I absorbed from the Funk and Wagnall's volumes, gave me quite an extensive vocabulary, and the uncanny ability to spell virtually any word that I could pronounce.

Years later, after returning to the States, I found myself in a small town high school in the eleventh grade, still cleaning aquariums, making backdrops for school plays, and photographing for the high school annual. I had also discovered rock music, met a couple of fellows that had electric guitars, and formed a band. Needless to say, my grades were nothing to write home about, and the letter "D" was a dominant feature on my report card. My parents made no fuss over it, because they knew of my talents in many other areas, but there sure was a shockwave of confusion at my high school when I, the ""D" student hippie fish hugger cartoonist kid, Won the High school spelling bee, over the seniors, nerds, brainiacs, and any other kid that stepped up to the podium..

Soon after, I had the opportunity to join the Cub Scouts. Our little troop met at our neighbor's home. After gluing some Popsicle sticks together and having a few cookies, we were informed that we were going on a camping trip.

My Mom said I could go, so I packed up some peanut butter, vanilla wafers, and my a.m. transistor radio. It was so little, and had one wire coming out with an earplug on the end. The Air Force bus was Bluebird blue, and I knew that because it said so on the front. The bus ride was long; we traveled uphill in a winding navigation, climbing upwards toward the mountain. We could look up, and see snow.

I knew this was no ordinary Cub Scout camping trip. I wondered if I had accidentally got onto the Marines bus.

The Bluebird came to a stop. A big man with a beard stood up.

"Here it is boys," he said, "Go find you a spot." I got off of the bus, and what I saw was mesmerizing. It was a lush, rolling forest at the base of a mountain; wooded, yet sparse enough to explore, with a beautiful stream flowing through. We also had a bunch of canvas tents in a pile. We pitched our tents on each side of the path that led to the stream and stuck our sleeping bags inside.

We then stood around a big fire, each taking our turn at burning marshmallows and hot dogs. The next morning, I woke up freezing and shivering. My sleeping bag was frozen too. The bearded man was standing in the snow, in his long john underwear, drinking coffee, while laughing out loud.

He saw me and yelled, "There he is!"

He then pointed at me. "You, go fetch me the bacon

stretcher!"

The grizzly scoutmaster gestured toward a tent where the food was stored. I went in looking for the implement, thinking that there must have been an oversight in planning somewhere.

I had no long johns, I had no blanket, and I felt like I was freezing to death. My toes and fingers were numb. I continued to search for the illusive apparatus, until I heard, "Come on out now, Lad," followed by a consort of laughter.

The bearded man poured some whiskey into his coffee, as I exited the mess tent.

"Where is the restroom?" I asked.

"Over there, behind the tree," he responded. I walked over to find a hole in the ground, with a roll of tissue hanging on a limb.

I opted out of that, went back to see about getting a ride home.

Suddenly, there were four Marines standing at attention in front of us few boys. They were in survival commando mode, and one had a chicken leg hanging out of his mouth. One by one, they grilled us boys harshly, teaching us how to survive in the wilderness.

One instructor took us to the brook, where he had made a snare to trap fish that were swimming upstream. Another showed us the edible parts of trees, and the location of water in plants for nourishment.

The third Marine taught us how to camouflage ourselves, and our sleeping places, as to not be discovered by the enemy.

The fourth one picked up a chicken and bit its head off. He held it up; drinking the blood that was pouring out of its neck, while allowing some of it to run down his chin.

The Scout leader poured some more whiskey into his coffee.

I endured the cold until later that day when a bus pulled up to the site. I told the bearded man I wanted to get on that bus.

"Go ahead, Lad," he said, as he laughed robustly.

So onto the bus I went, and we headed down the mountain, winding through the forest toward home. The skies had become dark, and there were only three of us on the bus, the driver, a kid sitting behind him, and myself, in the very back. I pulled out my little AM radio, placed the earplug in my left ear, and tuned in to The Far East network station.

It seemed like hours went by rumbling along toward the base. I decided to lay down, and I turned up my radio. I could see the stars through the windows as the lights from the flight line passed by.
A song I had never heard before came through my little earplug:
"A long, long time ago, I can still remember how the music used to make me smile…"
We drove around the flight line, as the song captivated my imagination.
We arrived at the housing compound as "the lovers cried and the poets dreamed." I got off the bus around midnight, walking home while hearing how the music died.

It was 1973, and I was 12 years old.

Going Home

March, 1974

One day we got to come home. It had been almost five years since I left the house on the hill, and I was twelve by then. We got there after dark, and I felt happy to be back home. Up the gravel hill, off Lewisburg Road, we pulled in the driveway. I ran down the walkway to the house. It was just like before, the fireplace was burning, and Berthie had biscuits and supper ready. I looked to see if the cat clock's tail was still swinging after all this time, and it was. There was also a hospital bed where the couch used to be.

My Aunt Shirley asked, "Do you want to see your Papaw? He's been asking for you." She nodded toward the bed. I felt a fear run through me. He looked so tired.

"Hey Papaw," I said, trying to stay strong. We spent some time talking and drawing pictures. I made sure he did not see me crying. The next morning Grandma Berthie told me he had gone to live with Jesus. I said it was ok because I knew that He loved Jesus. I also knew that Papaw loved me, and I loved him.

Right away daddy took us away again, to live in Chattahoochee. Grandma Berthie had to live alone, but Two Mamas across the street always kept her company. She loved fried chicken, especially from that man that was a Colonel. One day, Berthie wanted her fried chicken, and decided to drive into town and get it. While Grandma was gone, a huge tornado came and swept across Lewisburg Road from Two Mamas' house, and then up the hill. Momma and I drove back from Chattahoochee to help Grandma.

There were policemen in the streets and told us that we could not pass. Momma told them who we were, so they let us go through. It looked like everything was destroyed. There were a lot of lights at Two Mamas' house, and the police told Momma that they found her body on the other side of the highway. Two Mamas was gone.

I refused to look up toward the house on the hill, instead choosing to look ahead of us as we drove up the gravel road and into the driveway.

The tornado took out a swath straight through. The apple trees were gone. Papaws tub and shed were gone. I ran down the concrete walk to the house on the hill. There were trees and things everywhere, but the house was gone. There were two small walls still standing from the kitchen, and I looked over at them. The cat clock had stopped at 2:15.

And just like that, everything was gone.

LIFE OF COONIE

I found an old cell phone that I had misplaced last summer, and was excited to find a trove of photographs and video clips. Most were taken during the early days of my tenancy with my best friend and resident raccoon I had fondly named "Coonie". I cannot describe how intelligent this fuzzy little fellow was, nor how entertaining he could be. I also forgot how tiny he was back then, as evidenced in these pics.

I remembered the day I happened to be travelling toward my father's home in the country, when I spotted what appeared to be a black kitten struggling to cross the highway, dragging his back legs somewhat. As I pulled my little motorhome over onto the shoulder of the road, I saw him quickly disappear into the patch of thick clover that flourished alongside the paved county thoroughfare.

I glanced around for an item or two that I might be able to fashion into an entrapment device or containment enclosure, and all that could be mustered up was a small soft-sided ice cooler bag with a zipper top, a button-up shirt, and a small broom. Taking the broom in one hand, and the shirt in the other, I embarked on my impromptu wildlife recovery and rescue mission. Gently raking the top layer of the clover, I quickly exposed the elusive transient, albeit he was none too happy about my intervention into his attempt at eluding capture, waving his little paws at me and offering his best attempt at a menacing snarl.

At that point the little rascal's sharp teeth came into view, and I realized this was no beanie baby that I was dealing with. It was a baby raccoon, and as the cars kept whizzing by, I knew that the situation must be dealt with swiftly, as time was of the essence; at any moment this tiny masked refugee could scurry down into the ditch, or worse, back onto the highway in the path of oncoming traffic. My naturally empathic nature prompted me to offer a few words of apologetic assurance to my soon to be prisoner.

"It's o.k. buddy, I have to get you out of here" was followed by the large shirt landing on top of his canopy of concealment. In a flash, I scooped him up by wrapping the cloth around him, followed by rapidly shuttling him into the cooler bag. My adrenaline was flowing like I had just made an unwanted bungee jump, as I held the top of the canvas tote and closed the two zippers that originated on each side of the lid and came together in the middle.

Placing the package inside the motorhome on the engine cover seemed to be the best choice during transport, as I surmised that I could keep an eye on him and the road at the same time there.

The song, "On the road again" came to mind, and as we travelled down the highway toward my father's house, I started singing it aloud. He must have enjoyed the singing, because the bag started wiggling a bit, and every so often, a bulge would appear on one side or another as he was moving around inside.

I thought to myself that he might need some air, so I reached over, unzipping the two zippers apart about a half of an inch. There must have been a small beam of light enter into the abysmal darkness of his claustrophobic quarters, and freedom foremost on his mind, as I looked over to see three tiny, well-articulated fingers work their way through the zipper, one making room for the other, then another, until his whole hand had reached the outside.

In short order, the clever absconder wrapped his hand around the zipper tab, and began un-zipping the top off the bag, setting himself free. I panicked, yelling, "No Coonie!"... (I suppose that is when I named him), and lunged over to prevent the escapee from succeeding, while the track of the motorhome veered menacingly off to the right side of the road. My captive passenger cowered back, as I turned back toward the windshield, in view of the oncoming guardrail that lined the outer corners of the creek bridge. Instinctively, I gave the steering wheel a calculated jerk, compensating for the unfortunate shift in direction, but not without experiencing the shift in weight that often accompanies a momentous occurrence such as the one we were currently involved in...

Our re-directed path was slightly overcompensated, and the bag hosting my little hostage rolled over, spilling him out into the floorboard. I was still feverishly reacting to correct our vehicular miss-guidance and get our rolling domicile under control, as my hairy little passenger attempted to keep his balance by digging his claws into the carpet, his eyes wide open, as if in anticipation of an impending impact. Assorted items were flying off the shelves and crashing all about, which added to the sense of calamity and chaos.

The errant motorhome quickly straightened out, the ride returning to the once smooth conveyance that was present prior to our unfortunate altercation, and I slowly depressed the brake pedal, ultimately turning into the driveway of our destination. Stopping at the entrance to the estate, I placed the vehicle in park, and rubbed my eyes, trying to regain my composure. I turned and looked over at the engine cover.

There he stood, still with a white-knuckled grip on the carpet, eyes wide open, staring at me, and I swear that if I could have read his mind, I believe he would have said,
"Now what in the Heck was that all about?"

I knew the day would come, but I chose to ignore the inevitability, instead I opted to simply enjoy the time we were able to spend together. My friends would comment, "You know he is going to grow up, don't you?", and, "When he gets older he won't like you as much"... Those comments didn't dissuade me; I still ran his bath water, air-fried is popcorn shrimp, and put up with him waking me up late at night by tugging on my earlobe. He was determined, driven, and never gave up until I surrendered, and succumbed to his demands by getting out of bed to make him a snack. He was spoiled, but so was I. I always had a friend to talk to, and he always listened, sometimes intently, and other times remotely, but he always listened, and I never got tired of saying his name.

    He loved to pick things up with his hands, and feel different shapes and textures, and eventually learned how to turn the sink faucet on and off, and even get into the refrigerator.

    One day, after breakfast, he washed his hands and went over to the entry door of our little motor home. The two of us had shared that space since I rescued him as a baby over a year prior, and as he looked out the doorway toward the thick patch of bamboo, something caught his eye. That's when it happened...My best little friend then stepped off the slide-out step, walked toward the rear of the camper and turned the corner, leaving my line of sight.

And just like that, He was gone.....

And I sure miss the heck out of him...

THE SHEPHERD OF THE SEAS

I stood out on the beach, hoping to get a glimpse at God, I knew he was busy, but I thought that if I watched close enough, I may be able to catch him between works, if only for a brief moment in time, and perhaps, if my timing was right, he might see me,.. He might pause,… and see me….and he might even wave at me….

."Probably not today, though," I thought, because the sun was beginning to set, and the colors among the clouds were blending and changing. Brilliant hues intertwined, flowing effortlessly across the sky, and I could almost see his brushstrokes, as the Artist of all creation maintained his moving masterpiece. My eyes focused on the tiny sliver of light that was once the sun, disappear from my sight, as I witnessed what appeared to be a dark, rumbling, stampedic herd out on the horizon.

The illusion dissipated momentarily, then re-formed closer toward the shore, and then again, the pull of the moonbeams beckoning the waters closer, the fluidity of the salty solution providing a delicate shifting of possession between the gravity of mother earth, and the persuasive allure of the elusive moon. The lunar attraction gained strength, the wave building upward to its crest, the force of the tides toppling its peak, until the aquatic mass crashed over itself, churning into the surf like a boiling cauldron, then surging toward the shore in a panicked attempt at escape from the bondage of aquatic adherence.

As if reaching out with its last ounce of strength, the scattered remnants of what was once a mighty wave struggled to advance onto just one more inch of thirsty sand, as Gods hands reached out, raking his precious life giving serum of salinity back into containment, the great shepherd of the seas remaining vigilant, continually patrolling the water's edge for more errant ebbing, …

The stars were out by his time, and I turned to walk to my truck. Just as I turned, something made me pause and look back. A shooting star then fell from the sky, as if it was meant to catch my attention exclusively. I stared up into the heavens, slowly raised my hand, and waved back….

THE EAGLES OPUS

It is a special kind of feeling to be one with nature, to not merely witness the beauty of the beach estuary, but live it as well. To not just be a spectator on this earth, but be a child of it also; to see sunsets not as endings, but instead a celebrational reflection on the gift of today. The more one comes into tune with nature, the more one may appreciate the peace that may accompany it. I found this to be true and had nestled into my comfort zone at the little beach motel.

The tides would come in, then recede. Flocks of pelicans departed toward Saint Joseph's Bay in the mornings, only to return before sunset, gliding north toward Crooked Island sound, where they nested. The daily schedules of nature and my life there seemed to meld into a harmony, and I felt peace.

One day I paused for a moment, looking off the back deck toward the ocean. There were seagulls diving for small fish along the shore. One of the birds was successful, and flapped its wings toward the beach, depositing its prey upon the sand for mealtime. I found myself awe-struck, as I saw an American bald eagle swoop down, grasp the fish in its talons, and fly away.

The majestic bird turned, heading back in the opposite direction. I had seen an eagle's nest just east of Canal Park recently, and assumed it was the nest where he flew from.

It is visible from the bend, toward the north. It is a lone cypress tree, towering out of the swampy wetland area. One can see a woven basket of sorts nestled securely in the vertex of the remaining branches.

I thought that he must be feeding some hatchlings. Twenty or so minutes later, the majestic predator returned. He spotted another fish that the seagulls had brought ashore, quickly confiscating that one as well. The great bald eagle took again to the skies, circling around in gentle flight, as if to be the master of the clouds, heading back toward his nest among the wooded canopy.

On the top of the tallest tree lay his sanctuary of straw, the home fortress for the king of the birds. The carrier came to rest on a large limb, depositing its prey into the thatched loft. Three small fuzzy heads popped up, while the mother eagle began shredding the fish for mealtime.

Every morning, Atticus the Great would repeat his flights along the shoreline, in search of food for the hatchlings. As the days passed, two of the offspring grew larger, while one remained smaller than the others. The two larger eaglets grew into confidence, looking toward the sky, while the underling of the trio tended to look over the edge of the nest, feeling a sense of peril.

Through time, the maturing youngsters gained their feathers and on occasion, they would attempt to take flight. The smaller eaglet would try to flap his frail wings along with the others.

"Look at the runt," said one, "like he thinks he's going anywhere." The other responded, "Of course he's not. Why, he is no bigger now than the shell he was born in."

The two verbal aggressors enjoyed their laugh, while their scorned sibling stewed, his hairy eyebrows curling downward.

Then he responded defiantly, "I am Opus, Son of Atticus, king of the skies!"

"Perhaps so," one responded, "but can you do this?"

The boasting birds jumped off the edge of the nest, spread their virgin wings, and flew away, while young Opus cowered back into the security of his haven of twigs.

The winged patriarch had returned from his daily mission, perching himself on the high branch.

"What is to be of my son?" he wondered, "A storm is approaching. We must leave here."

The winds became stronger, as the brewing tempest drew nearer and nearer to the shoreline. The tallest trees were no match for the storms velocity; some yielding readily to the forces of natures fury, others resisting defiantly, only to be defeated by the barrage of gusts that came relentlessly ashore, each one seemingly stronger than its predecessor, and dwarfing all that were prior…

The tightly woven nest began to unravel, its well-placed reeds taking flight one by one, until the apprehensive eaglets home was in danger of dismantling completely.

The Great Atticus continued to plead with his son to find the strength to take flight, yet the smallest of the offspring remained consumed with fear. The once mighty pines continued to succumb to the forces of the winds, as the point of no return drew nearer. The Great Bald Eagle looked to the seas and knew then that he had no choice. Atticus the Great then paused, and looked into his sons eyes one last time before he took to the skies... The frightened eaglet was jostled about, as the nests last straws dislodged from their woven limbs.

High in the sky, the protective father circled around in predatory fashion, keeping a keen eye on the lone cypress tree far below. The winds were howling like a pack of hungry wolves, as the great eagle dove down toward his target, and with surgical precision, clenched his son in his talons, plucking him from the remains of his straw sanctuary. The mighty eagle then flew away, carrying his rescued cargo with him, as the last remnants of the thatched nest were consumed by the cyclonic winds.

The tornadic tempest disrupted the rescuing bird of prey, as a fragment of flying debris struck its left wing, causing one talon to lose its grip.

"Opus!" the great eagle shouted, "My son, save yourself! Fly! Fly away, now!"
The second talon soon lost its hold as well, as the sky king was sucked into the cyclonic chaos. The adolescent eaglet began spiraling downward, falling ever so rapidly, as the forest floor came closer into his sight. Spinning out of control, he began to lose consciousness. In a hazy dreamlike state, the winged patriarch's only son saw a vision of his father in majestic flight, soaring across the vast skies into an eternal sunset.

"Father!" He screamed...

Then, a voice echoed through his mind,

"Opus; my time has come, but you must be strong, face your fears; and conquer them. The sky is yours, it is your destiny and your frontier.. Be free, opus, spread your wings, and fly!""

Suddenly, his eyes opened, as the young eagle's wings spread out for the first time. The air currents quickly slowed his rapid descent, his aerodynamic frame gaining lift, his wings flapping clumsily.

"I'm flying!" he thought, "I'm actually flying!"

The young Opus, Son of Atticus the Great, then flew out of the storm's path, soaring across the treetops like he was indeed,

The "King of the Skies"....

The Imminent Predators

I find myself living in a realm of desolation and destruction.
Life is surreal for the most part; I must stay strong,
for the wolves are already at our door,
and the vultures are circling not far above.

My name is Jon Culver. My family and I rode out the hurricane of the century, while taking shelter in a small bathroom at the center of our home. We lived in a small cabin, about four miles north of the beach.
There, the storm made landfall, and proceeded to come directly over us. We lived off a dirt road, on the edge of a large, dense forest. As the storm approached, the skies became dark, then the winds began whipping by with such intensity, that the tall pines were lying over in a curve back toward the ground. The walls of our little cabin began to shake. The roof started to lift off in places, then fall back down again. "Into the bathroom!" I exclaimed, as I heard the trees begin to break over.

I grabbed a mattress off the bed, and wrestled it through the hallway into the bathroom. My wife, Ann, myself, and our two children, Jeremy and Beth, huddled in the steel tub, as I draped the mattress over us. The winds became more intense, and for the next forty-five minutes or so, we thought that we could die at any moment. We four held each other in such tight embrace; no wind could have possibly torn us apart. Beth, a mere 4 years old, began praying aloud.

The winds subsided, and we emerged from the little cabin. The pine trees were broken over as far as we could see; the smaller trees uprooted.

Debris lay everywhere, and part of our roof had blown off. I walked out toward the road to further survey the damage.

The power lines were down, and the road was inaccessible. I knew then, that it would be a long time before help came.

We immediately went into survival mode. Ann and Beth began rounding up candles, batteries, and taking inventory of food, while Jeremy and I went to get the generator out of the shed. I rolled the generator near the door, and filled it up with gasoline. I then ran an extension cord to the refrigerator, informing Ann,

"We must run this in increments, as to keep the food from spoiling."

I had close to five gallons of gasoline; we had to make it last.

Darkness came, and I started the generator once more. Taking a lamp from the living room, I set it on the table, then ran another cord to the generator. I told the children,

"After dinner, we have to turn this off, so we can have a candle party."

That seemed to calm them somewhat.

Outside, I had fashioned a cooking area, with a gas grill, charcoal grill, and a small table where I placed a pot for rinsing things off, along with a gallon of water. Above, I had hung two fluorescent lights that I had procured from the shed.

Along the rear of the property lay the edge of the dense forest. Last year, we had planted a large garden, in rows, from one end of the yard to the other. It hosted two rows of tomatoes, and one each of squash, cucumbers, eggplants, and garlic. The storm did not seem to affect it much, except for the debris lying about.

I fired off the grill, opened a beer, and reflected for a moment. My thoughts were convoluted, as it was difficult to grasp the reality of what had just happened.

"We are alive, and that is all that counts," I reassured myself.

I sent the children on a scavenger hunt for playing cards and such,
to entertain them in the realm of no electricity.

Ann harvested a few vegetables from the garden, while I looked around.

It was so dark by then; there were no streetlights, no moon, and no familiar glow on the horizon from the lights of Mexico Beach. The world, as I saw it, lay in total darkness.

My makeshift fluorescent lighting allowed me to see the garden, but beyond it lay the now invisible tree line. I handed Ann the plate of food and shut the generator off.

I opened another beer and lit a tiki torch. The candles were glowing inside, as the generator stopped running. I took a sip, and thought I saw a light in the woods; a small spark of sorts. I glanced back, around, and saw it again for a brief moment. One light reflection became two, as I witnessed the iridescent eyes peering out from behind the shadows.

They were focused directly on me.

I stood still.

"What is that?" I thought, "Too big for a cat or dog. Hmm."

I deduced it must be a coyote, so I grabbed my flashlight, focusing the beam toward the woods.

In a split second, I saw it. Two fiery eyes focusing on me, and me alone, non-blinking, non-wavering. Suddenly, they disappeared. It looked like a large wolf. I hurried inside the cabin, walking past Ann and the children towards the bedroom.

"What is wrong, Jon?' she asked.

I opened my closet door, pulled out my .375 magnum revolver, and secured it on my hip.

"Nothing dear, just taking precaution," I said, as I kissed her on the cheek.

Later that night, I wrote in my journal;

"They seem to be more prevalent at night. I could see them just beyond the tree line, their glowing eyes piercing through the darkness in sinister fashion, shrouded by the foliage and the dense fog. Some of them will stay still, their attention focused on you, never blinking, while the others move to the left and right. The moving ones are to be watched more closely, for they slowly pace back and forth, as if planning their eminent attack."

It was a long, hot night inside the little cabin, yet the breeze flowed through the broken-out windows, across the bed, and up through the missing part of the roof. I couldn't take my thoughts off of the images I had witnessed earlier; the glowing eyes that lay just beyond the tree line, peering menacingly at me through the darkness.

I made no note of it to the children, while my wife and I prepared the family's sleeping arrangements for the night.

"Hey, kids! It's slumber party time!" I announced, "Everybody pile in, and snuggle up!"

The giggles abounded, and stories were told, while my little family huddled together in the dark stillness of the night, the moonbeams shining eerily through a large hole in the roof above. We each in turn began to drift off to sleep, and I had found myself in a dreamlike state, when the solitude was broken by my daughter, Beth.

"What if it's a vampire, daddy?" she whispered.

"Beth!" exclaimed her mother, "Honey, there's no such thing as vampires. Isn't that right, Jon?"

"Umm, yeah," I responded, "That's only in the movies, Baby."

The next morning, I walked over to a neighbor's house, borrowed a bear trap, and set it up by the tree line, chaining it to a large stump.

It was just before midnight, and the children were tucked away in bed, their mother asleep by their side. Sleep came upon me once more, the deepest of slumbers; offering a subconscious escape from my perception of reality…..My mind was drifting, as I floated away into a sleepy abyss. There was a tree-line at the edge of a forest, The moonlight illuminating through the branches, casting shadows upon me..

A fog began to settle, its mystical weightlessness hanging gently in the air…I heard a rustling noise, and quickly turned toward the source. The midnight fog churned, as the short currents of air exhaled from the creature's nostrils….

I was encompassed with fear, as I made eye contact with the beast, the spawn of the devil himself, lurking in the shadows.

Its lust for blood was evident in its labored breathing… A low snarl emanated from its jowls, as saliva dripped profusely from the tips of the creatures fangs...

"Jon! Wake up!"'" I heard, as I was jostled back into the world of the wakened. It was my wife, Anne. "You were having a nightmare," she offered, as she reached over to comfort me. I took her in my arms, and lay her head on my chest, where she soon fell back asleep.

I lay awake next to her and the children, listening out like a radar at any possible sound emanating from the forest. It started as a rustling, or maybe not. I could not discern, but I could not lay there anymore either.

I quietly walked outside toward the garden, and paused. The sounds of the insects were like a symphony, and I found myself carried away by it. Then, in an instant, everything went silent. I heard a loud snap of a steel spring, then a vicious howl unlike anything I had ever heard.

I turned toward the noise, to see the large creature lunging out from the forest, heading straight for me, its shrieking was in resemblance to a panicked zombie, It's glowing eyes afire; its fang laden jaws gaping wide open. The beast was not of this world.

I turned to run, quickly losing my balance on the damp ground, then falling face first into the dirt. Suddenly the chain became taught, and the creature stopped abruptly, while falling into the vegetable garden. There, it began writhing uncontrollably, and the shrieks became softer. The beastly banshee wallowed through the garlic bulbs, slowly coming to a stop right at my feet.

The beast was dead.

A patrol car meandered around the broken trees and downed power lines, turning into the driveway.

"It's back here!" I exclaimed, "In the garden."

The beams from our flashlights were our only guides through the darkness, as we arrived at the snare. I was frozen in disbelief at what I saw.

A rickety, dried up framework of a canine skeleton, its skin stretched taught from bone to bone, its hair reduced to a few small patches, its eye sockets long empty.

"Mr. Culver," The deputy explained, "we don't have time for prank calls. What, did you find this under your shed or something?"

"No!" I pleaded, "This beast was trying to kill me!"

The irritated officer shook his head, "Jon, this animal has been dead for years. And just how did this tomato stake get stuck in its chest?"

"It must have fallen on it when it jumped out of the woods," I offered. We were interrupted by the sound of a two-way radio, signaling the patrolman of yet another call to duty. I watched the police cruiser drive away; the aroma of scattered garlic pungently apparent in the air.

PARANORMAL ACTIVITIES

This is a memo I made to myself a few years ago, to document what I perceived as paranormal activities that I personally witnessed during my fifteen-year residency at the aging inn. I remember posting it then, only to be asked repeatedly to remove it.

July 21, 2014

Last June, a lady checked in to #2, then came up to the office after about fifteen minutes and said, "I am sorry, I can't stay here, there are paranormal spirits in the room."

I asked if the room was in order, and she told me it was fine, but we desperately needed to contact someone to exorcize the spirits from there. Her husband agreed with her. She said some churches offer these services, or we can get a Native American priest to do it.

Guests most commonly complained about the sound of furniture moving around in the wee hours.

Last July a couple was staying in #5 and came into the office stating someone kept walking by their room, casting shadows, but no one was there. They were both convinced of a ghost of some kind.

Another guest was in #4 and told me that they turned off the bathroom light and went to bed. Soon after, they said the light turned back on somehow. They got up and turned it off, and went back to bed. A few minutes later, it came back on a second time.

Last year a guest in # 6 said they felt someone walking through their room.

Sometimes when I am the only one in the building, I hear someone in one of the rooms making bumping noises. I go around to check them all and to find no one there.

I have had many instances where the guests staying in #4 downstairs complain that someone above in #6 kept them up all night moving the furniture around.

In all of these instances, no one was staying in the room above, and upon inspection the furniture was indeed shifted out from their proper places.

About a month ago, my housekeeper came to me in tears saying that she was on the back deck around dusk, and while looking at the ocean, someone obviously barefoot came walking up behind her. As she turned around, there was no one there. She claims two other incidents where she felt a presence in the rooms.

On two occasions, I have been awakened by someone knocking on my apartment door that separates my apartment from the office. I got up, and checked to find no one anywhere.

Last week, I was awakened around three a.m. to a voice about five or six feet from my bed saying,

"Hello."

I jumped up, only to find no one.

Now, on October 31, 2019, on All Hallows Eve, shall the true story finally be told...

THE GHOST OF THE BUENA VISTA

Upon notice by a few select individuals of the proprietary nature, there came to pass an interest in an area along the shore, for the purpose of settlement, adjacent to the harboring comforts of Saint Joseph's Port.

This village began modestly, offering a retreat for even the weariest of worriers; a soon to be haven for sea fishers, sun seekers, and escape artists, lending itself to the propensity of the locals to frequent the taverns, while engaging in the imbibery and debauchery that resided therein.

And as it were, the days of life in the little hamlet by the sea became perpetual as the tides. The timely regimen of the waves, the daily repetition of sunrises and sunsets, and the temperature of the seasons had manifested quite a bustling of local residents, or "natives" as they might boast, over a pint or two.

The wealthy gypsies would build encampments along the shore, and then gather together, establishing councils, and departments, in order to subject themselves to self-discipline, while ensuring that others do the same.

I professed none other than to be a modest innkeeper, a wearied soldier of fortune harboring the remains of a misspent youth, seeking peace and solitude during my remaining days on this earth. And as it were to be, the circumstances were so, that I might remain host at such inn, for a period that offered time to write essays and reflections in a diary, To keep one as such for reference to others.

Whilst upon this notion, the little hamlet by the sea experienced a tempest of a lifetime's proportion, A violent storm to surpass all others. A climatic event of a climactic nature, seemingly to come out of nowhere, forever changing the lives of all that lay in its path.

Upon the small inn had been bestowed a spirit; a re-occurring presence of a lost soul. And as was sensed by many a guest over the years, 'twas a restless apparition, obsessed with relocating the furnishings in the wee hours of the night, closing doors, or casting shadows about to remind us of her presence.

One pleasant afternoon, upon notation of my random scribblings pertaining to the scurrying about of the human populace, I compared them to the ghost crabs. I was sure that each one thought that they had a purpose in what they were doing, when indeed the larger picture just portrayed a noisy, hurried confusion.

It was upon this relinquishment that I surrendered my attentions to other matters, and began spending time behind a simple easel, maintaining certain postures; in hopes of transferring witnessed or imagined images onto taught frames of canvas.

It was during one enlightened session that I began experimenting with the notion of "depth of field," or the use of points of infinity to indicate proximity of objects in relation to others. In this pursuit, I found myself on the edge of the highway, with pencil and ruler in hand, while staring down the road as far as my eyes could discern. The lines met at the vanishing point.

It was then that I saw it; a small horse drawn wagon, its size increasing proportionately as it drew nearer. 'Twas a wooden assemblage, twice as tall as it was wide, with large stagecoach wheels in its surround. There were cubbies, doors, and drawers all about, while pots, pans, and utensils of every type hanged and clanged alongside. A single carthorse was alone in its tether, yet the pace was a fitting match for the aging steed. At the front was a splintered board forming a bench of sorts, While at the reigns sat a seasoned fellow in weathered clothing, entrusting the remainder of his perch to a large yellow Labrador Retriever; and as note would be of it on my witness, the Canine was far more sober than his human counterpart…..

As fate were to have it, the wayfaring strangers came to a stop in front of the modest inn, followed by the dust emanating from the equestrian's worn and weary hooves. The driver pulled back his reigns, and clumsily placed the leather straps into their appropriate holsters.

His furry accomplice fidgeted profusely, as if to be in great need of dismount.

    The libatious traveler was none other than Archibald Cox, famed philanderer, purveyor of medicinals and potions, teller of tales, and quite the reputed cook. The visitor carried an air that his every utterance was indeed true and correct, while anyone attempting to question him would be hard pressed to prove otherwise.
    As a man indoctrinated into the polite art of greeting procedures, I welcomed the stranger in a manner that would please even the most road worn traveler.
    "Four pence a night for bed." I stated, "two pence for the horse, and two more for potluck, unless you decide to fire up those pots of your'n."
    "Consider it done, Lad!"
    "Pogo, get the rope!" replied his master.
    Pogo wore a harness of leather strapping, not unlike the belt that held up mine own breeches. The attentive canine went to the back of the wagon, and retrieved a large bucket containing a coil of rope and a fishing net.
    "One more thing," I added; "wear not your boots to bed, for hell will fall on you from the keeper of the house."
    "Similar in nature to my last visit, I'm sure," he laughed.
    I smiled and held out my hand, "Good to see an old friend. What brings you here?"
    "Rumor has it that you harbor a haunting, Sir;" he stated, adding, "I have been reputed to dabble in the arts of exorcism, having successfully purged lost souls from many a dwelling, and body." The visitor then handed me the reigns, commenting, "I am here for the ghost."
    I watched Pogo run out across the beach to the surf.
    "What is he doing?" I asked.
    The apparitional abolitionist chuckled,
"Why, he's going fishing, Lad!"
    I walked down to the beach to investigate. The pup jumped into the water with the end of the rope, and swam out in a loop, drawing a net behind him. He paddled back, and brought it to me.

My friend and I pulled in the net, yielding a bounty of fish for our evening meal. As we prepared the kettle to melt the lard, we took turns filling our flasks from my ale barrel, while entering into a banterous volley of jokes, stories, and opinions.

The night skies were soon to pass, whence upon the stroke of midnight the humorous chatter turned to silence as my guest and I felt a strange presence in the room. We agreed to begin the process of removing the unwelcome spirit at the break of dawn.

At sunrise, the practitioner began pacing all about the inn, reciting verses and sipping on what appeared to be the finest of bitters. As the hours went by, the spirit became more and more agitated.

The skies became dark and the winds increased, as the eager eradicator performed his ritual of expulsion. Without warning, the skies erupted, as the clashing of good and evil consummated at the rage of the angry seas. The dwellings of men succumbed to the might of nature, as the waves came relentlessly, one after another, as if to be aqueous claws, ripping away the building and all that lay therein and then dragging the remains into the surf. The roof surrendered to the winds, taking flight toward the heavens; and we knew then, that we would be swept away.

Archibald Cox continued staring into the eye of the storm, shouting, "I command Thee, Spirit disperse! Be gone unto thine own journey!"

The floor began to move under my feet.

I shouted, "Pogo! Get the rope!"

Pogo fetched the end in short order, and I began tying myself to a cast column. The challenged spirit grew Omni presently stronger, while the howling of the wind echoed that of a bloodthirsty banshee. The floor collapsed into the sea, and I saw the helpless dog sliding downward, as if to be an appetizer for the carnivorous waves. So with last mustering of strength, I reached out, snaring the pup by its harness, while attaching the large brass ring to mine own belt-loop.

The furnishings took flight into the cyclonic chaos as the entire inn began disintegrating around us.

The imposering pastor commanded, "With all the strength the Lord retaineth in me, I command ye leave this place!"

As if in a retaliatory response, a demonic wave approached,

dwarfing all that were previous, and in a thunderous clashing, crushed the remains of the inn, consuming none other than Archibald Cox himself, carrying his body into the briny depths of his abysmal grave. I held on to Pogo as tight as I could, my vision depleted, my senses breached, our bodies flailing around at the mercy of the rope. It was then that I lost consciousness.

My thoughts convoluted into a swirling phantasmagoria of thoughts and images.

"Mama? Is that you?" I dreamed.

I was awakened by a loud voice, saying,
"You there! Are ye alive?"
I looked toward the street, the dog and myself hanging like a cocoon from the last remaining concrete pile.

"Yes, Constable," I replied, "Just a little tied up at the moment."

We were quickly rescued, and left to survey what little remained. Most of the village had been destroyed; the few remaining fragments of the inn were poking out of the rubble, and I spotted a small armchair.

I picked it up to set it proper; a lone chair, among the ruins, facing toward the sunset. I then heard a mumbling voice coming from the water's edge.

It was none other than Archibald Cox himself, hobbling up soaking wet from the sandy shore.

"Well, I guess we got that out of the way!" he boasted, "Another successful eradication to add to my resume."

"Yes, Archie, you did it; the spirit is certainly gone now," I said sarcastically. "And so is everything else."

We three survivors sat among the ruins looking out to the sea, and from the corner of my eye, I saw that lone armchair moving slowly across the sand…

160

QUARANTINED; DAY 15

I had settled into the reality of a self-induced quarantine; sequestering myself into the woods, among the remnants of the homestead that had been destroyed by Hurricane Michael a year and a half prior. Many mornings after the storm, I would arise, only to venture out into the land of the rebuilders, while thinking how strong my desire was to simply stay home, out of the chaotic scurry of the populace.

Now I had the time.
Now, I could fix that old lawnmower.
Now, I had the time to cut the thorn vines away from that choked out lemon tree.
Now, I had the time clean up the rest of the wind-blown debris from eighteen months prior; the subtle reminders of the storm that had so strongly challenged my faith and resolve.
I placed the battery charger cables on the old tractor, and checked the oil level.
"Oh, that's right," I thought, "don't forget to hook up the fuel pump wire," as it had been haphazardly rigged by a shade tree aficionado a long time ago.
The four-cylinder diesel engine fired off; the knocking sound and the smell of the oil a familiar comfort; reminiscent of days long ago. So, off I went, chugging along, pulling broken limbs, loading decaying boards into the bucket, scooping up piles of broken blocks. I was careful to navigate around the patch of clover, a large area adjacent to where my above ground pool used to be, a lush green habitat where I would see butterflies, green frogs, and "Georgia thumper" grasshoppers breed and thrive over the years.

I spotted a fallen tree limb on the edge of the bed of vegetation, placed the tractor in neutral, and dismounted my iron steed. Suddenly, I felt a sharp pain under my left kneecap; the weight of my body succumbing to gravity, as I tumbled head first toward the ground. The diesel engine was still running, as my body lay flat on its back, my head near the four-foot-tall left rear tire, the sharp pain persisting at every attempt to erect myself.

I glanced over to my truck, which happened to be where I had left my cell phone. I knew that I could not begin to reach it, so instead I focused on turning off the tractor. Another attempt at standing up was quickly rebutted, as I screamed in agony; accepting my fate that I would be there for a while.

Just within arm's reach was a broken limb. Picking it up, I could reach up to the rigged wire that fed current to the fuel pump. After a few attempts, I managed to snatch the wire loose, the four cylinder motor slowly shutting down from lack of diesel.

And there I lay.

I resigned myself to my apparent fate, and for the next two and a half hours, I saw the world from a completely different perspective. I noticed how the clouds were moving across the sky, propelled by the direction of the winds. I began to completely relax; my mind drifting away to memories from a long time ago; a little boy, lying in the grass, seeing shapes in the clouds. As I lay silent, something strange happened. I saw a new world open up to me, albeit on a tinier scale than I had ever perceived before.

I glanced over to my left, at a large anthill; large in the way that it was taller than I, as I lay on my back in the clover. The tiny soldiers were carrying particles of food up the hill, then disappearing into a portal that must have led deep down into the realm of their queen.

A scattering of bark flew off the branch above. It was a squirrel, apparently involved in an altercation with another. After a loud exchange of chatter followed by an apparent resolution, one conceded to the other, and they both parted ways.

A buzzing sound caught my attention; my head turning to the right. At first, I thought it was a hornet; which was a startling notion, because I had developed an allergy for their stings years ago, yet it turned out to be a simple mud-dauber; its long disproportionate legs dangling as it hovered harmlessly above. The sun was attempting to peek out through the dense leaves of the majestic oak tree, which was my only shelter from its rays. I then witnessed something moving up the rugged bark of the main trunk. It was a large grasshopper, maybe four inches in length, with long antennae reaching from its head to its hindquarters, its articulated legs resembling the long bows of a violin, prepared for the next concerto.

And there I lay.

    I let all of my self-induced worries flitter away just like the butterflies hovering above, as the afternoon sky started to fade.

    Then, in an instant, it began. A bullfrog bellowed, followed by another; a chorus of crickets chiming in, then the grasshoppers. A symphony of nature unfolded for me and me alone, as I had the front row seat in the bed of clover. A sense of contentment overcame me, as the sunset cast a multicolored aura across the horizon, the sun setting in a climactic conclusion to nature's concerto. I heard a vehicle pull into the driveway, and, as I waved out to my rescuers, I thought to myself how I didn't want it to end…

Maybe tomorrow, I will re-visit that little patch of clover, and once again;

    There, I will lay.

QUARANTINE; DAY 23

The lingering effects that hurricane Michael had on my daily routine had begun to soften somewhat. Although I knew it would be years before things got back to what I used to perceive as normal, I found myself spending more time each day performing tasks without my mind constantly on the storm. "Could it be we finally get a break?" I wondered.

That notion was not to be, because about that time I received a phone call from my girlfriend, informing me that she was being placed under a mandatory quarantine for approximately three weeks. There was news about a pandemic sweeping across the globe at an alarming rate; Airports were being shut down, hospitals were overflowing. As she had recent heart surgery, she could take no chances, as this virus preyed on the most vulnerable of the populace.

Anywhere I went offered potential to come into contact with a carrier of the virus, so I decided to return to my camp in the woods and wait it out, at least until I knew that I had not been exposed, therefore could not transmit the virus to others.

I spent my time cleaning and organizing the workshop in the back yard, and looking forward to tackling the storage shed in the back, crammed full of boxes, broken tools, bags and bins of all kinds, stacked haphazardly on top of one another. Each item removed brought back memories, and it was quite an intriguing adventure as the containers revealed their contents.

As I continued to clear out the aging shed, I discovered my old train cars and buildings in a decaying foot locker. A long lost collection of toys, forgotten in recent years, yet I stood mesmerized; looking at each one of them, the memories taking me back to long ago.....A little boy, playing with his train set.

I carried the container into my camper, and grabbed my camera along with a wool blanket and a string of old Christmas lights. For the next few hours, I was teleported to a make believe place, as only my imagination and camera could portray it....

Welcome to the gunfight at Grimy gulch...

166

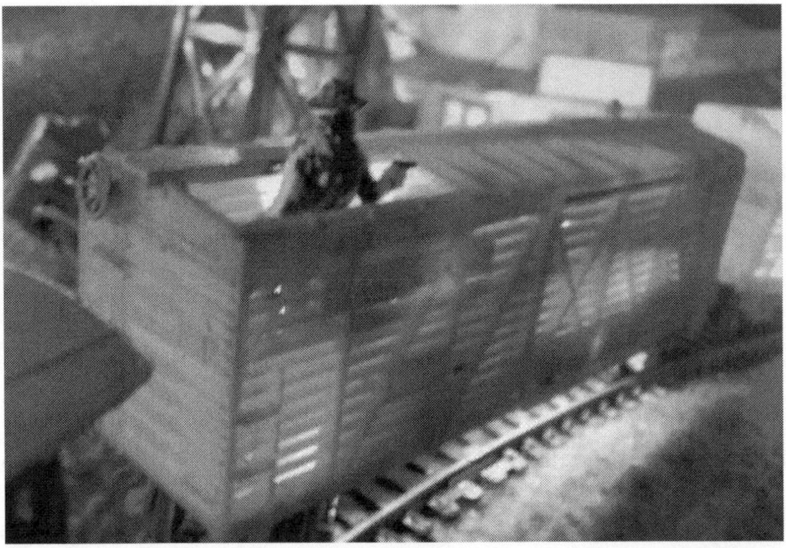

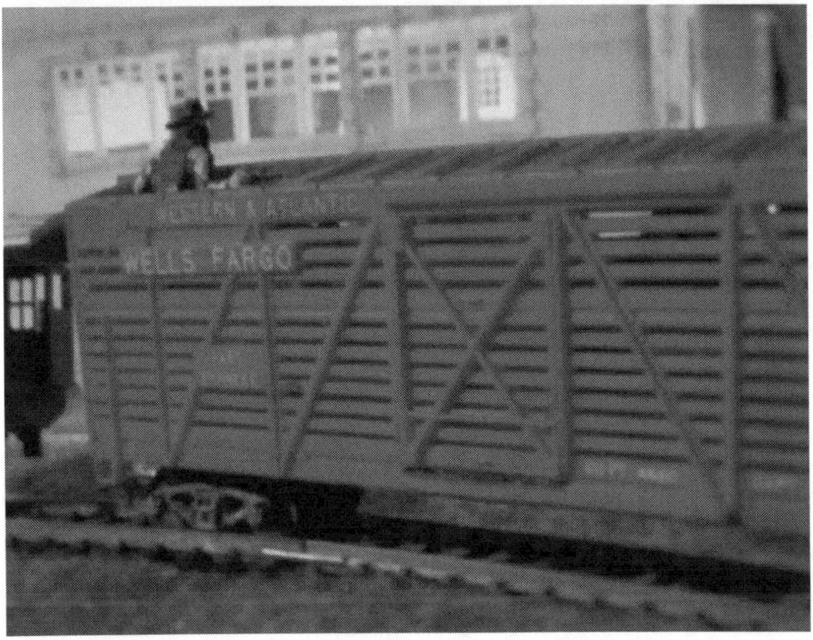
WESTERN & ATLANTIC
WELLS FARGO

168

A PLEASANT DISTRACTION

If we teach children to see the wonderment in this world; to appreciate the miracles in nature; they then may see the value of life, of the earth, and of the seas, and begin to comprehend the existence, and the power, of the creator of all that is around them.

It was the summer of 2020. I had finally sensed the notion that things were beginning to calm somewhat; that the chain of challenging events that tested my very faith and resolve would finally relinquish itself, like a raging surf conceding to the will of the tides, and returning to the placidity of a once calm sea.

The events of the past few years had taken quite a toll on me, so I had sought out a simpler way of life; one with a limited capacity for stress; one that offered time for reflection, reflection on a long life of applying myself to a regimen of hard work and over-obligation, only to see the results dissipate into the sands.

I had resigned myself to spending my days taking care of my aging father, as well as perform repairs on his home, which was still damaged by the effects of Hurricane Michael.

Having just finished applying another coat of drywall mud on the wall joints in the living room, I proceeded to head outside to wash out the mud pan. A car pulled up, and I saw my hired helpers arriving to join in the fun. With them, they had brought a young boy, maybe 12 years of age, and I greeted him with a handshake. I explained the scope of work to my eager employs and proceeded to get back on task. "Time to wash out this mud pan", I thought, as I approached the water hose spigot.

"I hate washing out mud pans," I continued on in my mind.

"I'll just drop it in a bucket of water and wash it later" I mentally concluded. I looked down to see two water filled buckets, each with my three other unwashed drywall pans in them, along with a half of a dozen drywall finishing knives, every one of them covered in snow white gypsum compound, and submerged in a milky, muddy mess. I placed the pan in the bucket, and turned toward the garage.

    The young boy emerged from the house, along with one of my hired helpers..."I'm going to have to take him home", she said, followed by, "He has no internet, his video games won't work here, and he's bored." I had a flashback to when I was his age, and reminisced about how things were back then, along with the many memories of the adventures I had encountered by simply going outside, exploring, and using my imagination. I tilted my head slightly, and with a voice similar to an Oompa Loompa, I said, "Bored?. Bored?"....."How can you be bored, with all of the amazing adventure around you?" I turned to my co-worker and stated, "Get to work, I got this...C'mon buddy"....
I led the impressionable young lad to my truck, where I procured my digital camera. "You see, "I informed him, "There are adventures all around us, some of them so small that we don't always see them. Let's explore."

    So, off we went, in search of critters and such to photograph. For the rest of the afternoon and into the evening, that child and I were mesmerized by the things we encountered, and boredom was nowhere to be found. We returned to the house after dark, announcing, "The expedition was a success!" and proceeded to download the photos onto the computer. There, I showed the young man how to center up and crop the images, enlarge them, and adjust the color levels and such. My juvenile apprentice was fascinated at the images we had captured on our journey through the garage and into the back yard, and as he left with the printed out photos he said to his guardian, " For my birthday, I don't want more video games...I want a camera just like Mr. Michael has."....

THE MESSENGER

Make your mission through life not one of self-gain, instead use your strengths to lead others into the light.....

And in the dream, he stood before God, asking; "Why his creator would sicken his own children, why would the Almighty send the rage of the storm to wash them away?"

The sky erupted into a swirling spectacle of colors, a visual tempest of unimaginable intensity. His eyes became blinded, the vision only for him to see. As the lights unfolded, he felt great pressure onto his ears, rendering deafness upon him.

Yet he felt the words so strongly that the vibrations became audible. The voice being omnipresent, it was as if the weight of a thousand souls lay upon his chest.

Then God responded,
"For I gave mankind intelligence, and mankind hath forsakened me, and mankind hath poisoned thine mother earth, and mankind hath continued to scourge, and mankind hath continued to kill. There shall be a third plight bestowed, a wrath unlike any other."

"No! My dear Lord, what can we do? How may we redeem ourselves?" he begged.

The powerful voice replied, "The salvation of man lies within you; for you are my messenger. Go forth and teach the word of God. Stop killing thine own planet. Stop killing and eating my creatures."

He felt a violent jostling, as he was abruptly awakened.

"Wake up, Jon!" spoke his attentive bedmate. He sat up erect, as if in a panic, breathing heavily into the midnight air, his brow wet with sweat. As his glassy eyes regained focus, he turned to his wife and said,

"We must inform the others."

TREASURE

"If your soul is fulfilled, your needs are few"

In my mind, I saw it as a rock; a concrete monument that had remained steadfast through the tests of time and the tempests of the seasons…..One of the original buildings constructed in the small town of Mexico Beach in the early1970's, The Buena Vista Motel had seen many a visitor in its forty plus years of operation.

I stood at the edge of the highway that morning, remembering a day in 1984, when my father and I took our newly acquired fishing boat out of the Mexico beach canal and embarked on our first attempt at braving the waters of the gulf. I remembered panning my vision along the coastline, and noticing that the "Wayside Beach Supply" (later known as Toucans restaurant), and the Buena Vista were the two tallest structures in town.

In 1995, Hurricane Opal, a category 3 storm, had destroyed many of the early beach cottages; the little block buildings built on concrete slabs, or wood frame cabins set up on wooden posts. The fall of the shanties had given rise to a new generation of vacation homes, built up higher, on long pilings imbedded deep in the sand. Still, the original motel stood vigilant and steadfast with the new arrivals, perched upon its hand-dug concrete columns, as if to make a statement to the others that "I was here first"…

"But that was back then", I thought, as I stood by the edge of what was left of the highway that morning. That is a morning that I will never forget; October 11, 2018. The day after the unimaginable happened. Hurricane Michael, a category 5 storm of massive strength and intensity, had hit us head-on. The newly built two and three story structures that had dwarfed the little inn were no match for Michaels fury; many of them ripped from their support piles, floating across the highway; the others washing out to sea, as their contents were blown inland, landing in the dense forestry to the northeast.

I glanced around at the debris that lie intermingled with the broken and crumpled trees; the roof sections, the broken furniture fragments, the crushed appliances. The scattered remnants of what were once beach homes littered the crushed forest, an unfitting graveyard for the refuges that offered so many memories, to so many visitors, for such a long time.

Turning back toward the sea, I tried to make sense of it all. I thought to myself, "She was the first building to fall." The storm surge had saturated the sand around the hand-dug pilings from 1974 so fast, that nothing in, or outside the structure had been blown across the highway. The building that I had called home for over 15 years must have imploded straight down, and was quickly consumed by the raging surf. All that remained were the two floor slabs, crushed like eggshells in the sand, and a few concrete piling fragments.

There was a lone object sticking up out of the rubble, a nail gun that my friend Dave had brought into the office for repair. I remembered that I had set it on the floor next to my desk, a week before the storm, as we were waiting on parts for it.

During the clean-up and removal of the debris, I stared intently at the excavator bucket as it made each scoop into the sand, hoping to find something else from my office or one of the guest rooms. At first, I was thinking of something I could keep as a souvenir, or maybe by a million to one chance, that the excavator's bounty would reveal a buried treasure; my safe I that I had mistakenly left behind when I evacuated. I remembered how it was sitting under the printer stand a few feet away from the nail gun. I spoke to no one about it, but kept a keen eye out for it, until the last bit of rocky material was plucked from the sand and raked clean...Nothing. Except for the twisted and mangled air fastener, I had failed to find one single item from the entire seven room inn, or its office and laundry area.

On many an occasion, I would scour the 14 acre parcel behind Gulf Foods, where the fragments of the other buildings and their contents were, hoping to possibly find the missing lockbox... Nothing. Not so much as a bar of soap, a towel, or even a piece of a roofing shingle, which was odd, because on many occasion, a slight wind would dislodge one of aging tabs and I would find it across the street in the parking lot of the grocery store.

Many months passed, and I would continue to keep a watchful eye on the area after the heavy rains and the erosion they caused.

Often, the storm waters would wash out trenches in the sediment leading from Gulf Foods parking lot onto the barren wasteland that was once the flourishing forest; and I held hopes that the weathers influence might help reveal the briefcase size box of cash. Nothing. Other than the nail gun, not a single item was ever found from the Buena Vista Motel....

It had been two years since the storm of storms, and the cleanup effort was nearly complete. Many people had begun to rebuild their homes, and the beaches and dunes had been re-nourished, yet I would still find myself on watch for the elusive little vault...one day while watching the sunset, I saw something from a distance at the water's edge, an indiscernible object among the bounty of freshly washed up seashells. As I got closer, I began to recognize something about it, yet was unsure what it was. A relic of sorts, a vague reminder of what used to be. In my mind, I navigated through the separate rooms that I had maintained, repaired, and rented for so long, until I pinpointed where and what it was. A lamp... yes!, a piece of the lamp that sat on the table in the office apartment! I carefully picked the pottery shard up and placed it into my truck.

Later, I went home to my camper in the woods, sat it up on a shelf, and reminisced... The memories came in like waves, one after another, gently receding like the waters of an incoming surf.

In the months that followed, I would find myself glancing at the relic from time to time, feeling a sense of closure and comfort, often followed by a nostalgic smile. I stopped looking for that safe after that; the little piece of broken pottery meaning more to me than a box of money ever could have,

For I felt that I had finally found my treasure....

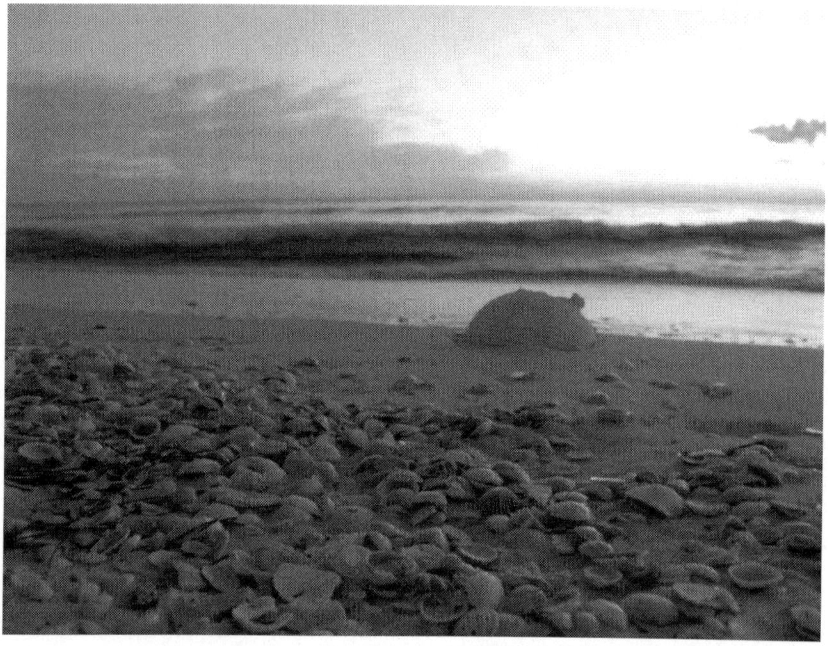

DAD AND JESUS

    I pulled off of the county road, just as I had done many times before, turning into the driveway where my parents had made their home…As I walked past the garage toward the house, my mind attempted to block out the visual of the random trash that lay about; the junk and useless refuse surrounding my peripheral vision. So many years had passed, so many reflections; "Once upon a time" could be readily found in a random box of old photos, or a simple glimpse at an aging Oak tree; any trigger to the memories of the past would release a surge of recollections; …some pleasant, some not so…

    I walked up the inclined ramp to the back door leading onto a small, enclosed porch; the closest access to the hallway hosting the entrance to the master bedroom. I had just built that ramp a couple of weeks ago, out of two long laminated veneer beams that I had planned to use at my residence just down the road. "Strange twist of fate" I thought, as I looked down at them. Not long ago, I had set them up on 6x6 posts, nailing them off about eight feet above the concrete slab, in anticipation of finally building a little workshop in my back yard.

    My life-long tendencies toward procrastination proved a benefit for once, as I neglected to follow through with the bolting process. When hurricane Michael unleashed its fury upon the little mobile home in the woods, it tossed down large pine trees as if they were toothpicks, inevitably causing two of them to land on the laminated beams. The few nails that held them in place gave way so quickly, one might think they saw the trees falling, and just before impact, went ahead and backed out on their own accord, as if to save themselves.

    I forced a slight grin onto my lips, realizing that if I had indeed bolted them off as I should have, they surely would have shattered in pieces at the weight of the massive pine trunk that lay amongst the storm debris that morning. However, there they were, serving a more noble purpose; a safe means of egress for my aging father.

    I could tell he was having trouble walking up even a few steps, much less four or five. His greatest nemesis, however, was the fourteen steps he tumbled down three months prior while visiting his

South Florida townhouse, a favorite get-away he and my mother used to frequent. The fall took a great toll on him, as he lay bedridden through the door on my right. He had a sign hanging on the doorknob, that said he was either "Cruisin" or "snoozin", indicating whether he was napping or not. I peeked through the crack in the door, as to not wake him..

I saw him lying there looking back at the opening between the door and the jamb, quickly saying "Yeesss?", as he usually did, when I would look in to check on him. No matter how quiet I attempted to be, he always knew that I was there. I even joked one day about it, asking him, "What, do you "smell me coming" or something"? He just smiled, and said, "I sensed it". Followed by, "I know when you are here".

"How are you today Papa? "I would ask.

"I'm in pretty bad shape", He responded, adding, "But I think I'll be completely healed in another two weeks" …

A couple of months prior, my 85-year-old father was in Tampa at his resort townhouse, and fell head-first down a flight of stairs. After a four-week stay in the hospital, and a considerable amount of time in a therapy-based nursing facility, he came home to Wetappo creek, where we lived approximately four miles apart.

That was 14 months ago, and since then, I had voluntarily became his sole caretaker, and rehabilitator, tending to his needs as well as the repair and maintenance of his 14 acre estate; which had not yet been repaired from the damage caused by Hurricane Michael. These tasks consumed all of my time, and I lost focus on my writing. I also lost parts of myself.

A few months after I arrived, he had reached a point of recovery where he used his crutches and walkers less, had regained his equilibrium, gained over ten pounds, and was feeling great. Even though he would still have his bad days, for the most part, he seemed to be content, and him and I got to spend some time together.

Dementia is a curious condition, sometimes you wonder if it is really there or not, and other times it takes over, and you find yourself speaking to a different person, one who appears lost within themselves, and somewhat confused.

It was early on in my tenure there that one day after scouring the classified ads; I drove to a mini storage unit and picked up the package. I got back to the house, and went into a secluded workshop in the back. There, I put it together, then waited. He had houseguests, and I did not want to wake them, so at approximately 2:30 a.m., I rolled it up the inclined ramp into to the house, pushed it over to his bedroom door, and slowly backed my way out.

The next morning I made myself scarce, and let his guests visit, but when I arrived, I was questioned by one of his old fishing buddies..."Did you leave this electric scooter here for your daddy?" he asked. I responded, "What Scooter? I don't know anything about it." For the next few days, he was everywhere on that little scooter, usually with the throttle wide open, and making a "wheeee" sound as he zipped by. The third day, I arrived back from an errand, and he was standing in the driveway with a stern look on his face.

"What's up, Papa?" I asked.

"I've given it a lot of thought, and I talked with the others, and, umm, I'm pretty sure that it was you that put this scooter at my door." He responded.

"Well," I said, "All I gotta say is, umm, a long time ago, there was this little boy, and every Christmas morning he would get up, and run downstairs. It was amazing, there were always bunches of presents for him, and it made him realize just how much he was loved.".... He looked at me puzzled for a moment, and I then said, "Merry Christmas, Papa".

He loved that scooter, and rode it all over the 14-acre parcel he called home, sometimes toting fishing poles to the creeks edge, or taking the high road to find me mending a fence, or cleaning up debris. As the days and months passed, I could tell he was getting weaker; the highs were always followed by the lows, and he was getting tired.

Fall had arrived, and the days had become welcomely cooler. One day, I went to his room to check on him. He was staring out the window, with a content look on his face.

"Whatcha doin' Papa?" I asked.

His next words surprised me, as I had never, in my 59 years of being around him, heard him speak of God, or any opinion on the existence or non-existence thereof.

He said, "I've been talking to Jesus today."

I responded, "That's great, Papa"..."What were you talking about?"... He turned and said,

"We have been talking about how everything is supposed to be, and how everything is going to go, and I know now that everything is going to be all right...."

I had never heard him speak of Jesus, and I found comfort in the fact that he acknowledged the existence of one who I had professed to him to be my savior many times in the past. Not long after, My father passed away, and I carry with me on this day, and for all of the days that follow for me on this earth, the belief that he was indeed visited by a holy presence that day, and that he embraced it, and for that one day, out of the scurry, hurry and chaos that encompassed his long life, he got to meet, and to speak,, one on one, with Jesus Christ, The son of his God......

CATEGORY EIGHT; A FICTIONAL PREMISE

It had been almost two years since "The storm" made landfall on the little beach town. It was referred to as "The hurricane of the century," by the locals, and the healing process had been well underway.

Often in life, unfortunate incidents can offer new possibilities; the new normal began to feel normal. Repair projects to the city's infrastructures were being completed, as businesses and homes were in the repairing or rebuilding process. My daily routine almost always included a trip to the local hardware store, where residents would interact, while exchanging greetings, gossip, and opinions.

Today's local scuttlebutt pertained to a tropical depression that was forming in the Atlantic Ocean. The low-pressure system was semi-stagnant, yet appeared to be on a slow east to west trek towards South Carolina. I thought to myself that this was farther above the equator than I remembered seeing prior hurricanes form.

Later that evening, I arrived back at my camper, and turned on the news. The forecaster eloquently explained the storms probable path, while also reporting conditions in other areas, including another small tropical depression approaching the Turks and Caicos Islands. I was then instructed to "Stay tuned, because sports was next."
I turned off the television.

The next morning at work, the job site banter was all about the possible hurricane. The path of the storm was unknown, and no mention was made of the little tropical depression farther below in the tropics.

The next morning, I turned on the news again and the weatherman was pointing across the radar image, while reporting, "Hurricane Damien continues to churn toward the North Florida coast, possibly intensifying into a category four storm, as tropical depression Miguel approaches the Florida Keys."

The camera turned and focused on the two news anchors.

"Wow, is there a possibility we might be affected by two storms at the same time?" inquired the perky young brunette.
"Highly unlikely." stated the meteorologist.

"Most depressions such as Miguel never gain much strength and Hurricane Damien will most likely lose momentum due its location and trajectory, far above the warmer air of the Gulf Stream."

I turned off the television, while mumbling, "Blah, blah, details on the half hour."

The next morning at the construction site, the discussions turned to the weather once more.

"Did'ja see that one little storm that was a' speedin' up?" chuckled Earl.

"Well, it ain't gonna catch Damien," he boasted.

The next thing I know, my two construction compatriots are betting on which storm makes landfall first. I just smiled and nodded.

We wound up at the bar later, and as the weather report was updated, so was the ante. It was a tight race, and as the "little storm that could" was proving itself, the larger storm was getting weaker. The boys continued to wager their money on their picks like it was a redneck road race. I laughed throughout the encounter, and then headed home.

I started wondering, "What if the two storms were to collide?"

3:04 A.M. Washington, D.C.

The Marine Guard stood in full saluted attention, as the quickly assembled delegation entered the White House. The pacing of footsteps was hurried, and few words were spoken. There was a slow turn of a doorknob.

"Mr. President," spoke the voice, "there is an urgent matter at hand."

The group quickly gathered in the Oval office.

"What is going on?" asked the leader.

The Chiefs of staff from the Pentagon were in entourage with senior advisers, a group of scientists, and a young intern from the local College. The Vice Admiral of the Navy informed him, "Sir, there are two separate hurricanes heading toward the coast of Florida. The current data indicates they will be of somewhat equal magnitude at their prospective landfall locations."

"Then we must prepare for both. Send twice as much help," was the decree. There was a short silence in the room.

The Vice Admiral stated, "Sir, There is one slight possibility. It is only theory, however."

The President nodded, responding, "Carry on."

"If certain atmospheric conditions change, the two storms might even take a track toward one another. It is possible that they could collide."

The head of the National Weather Service interjected, "Sir, if they indeed were to collide, the pressure and speed differentials should cause them to basically blow each other out."

The Brigadier General spoke up. "Sir, I respectfully submit that these considerations are ridiculous. There has never been an anomaly recorded such as they propose. It's basically not possible."

The Air Force Commander interjected; "I beg to differ. It is indeed scientifically possible, yet exponentially improbable."

The President glanced at the clock.

"What are you people talking about?" he exasperated, and turned to his top adviser.

"What do you make of this, Vice?" he asked.

"Sir, it is our duty to inform you of any and all threats to the United States, no matter how unlikely the odds."

The dignitaries became silent. The Commander in Chief looked over at the young intern, who had been fidgeting with the stack of files on her lap. She was glancing around the floor, but seemed to have the energy of a race car on a starting line.

The Attorney General Stood up and stated, "Sir, this is my daughter, Lisa. She is a student of meteorological sciences, and has quite a vivid imagination as well."

"Miss, is there anything you wish to tell me?" asked the President.

The young intern turned pale, as she rose up out of her chair, "Yes, Mr. President, there is." She opened her file, only to see the contents spill out onto the floor.

The young student bent down, nervously scooping the notes into a haphazard pile, while looking up sheepishly at her mentor.

The President stated, "Miss, you may bring your papers to my desk."

She approached, and laid her reports out for the Commander in Chief. "What is it, Young Lady?" He inquired curiously... The young student drew a breath, and with a hesitant air of confidence, began her dissertation.

"Sir, the system forming toward the north is unusual, as those temperatures rarely harbor hurricanes. The anomaly could be a possible result of the global warming phenomenon." She continued, "The temperatures from the jet stream could influence its rotation, resulting in a more southerly course; while the well-fed tropical depression to the south will certainly strengthen if it continues on its current path."

A voice came out from behind. "Sir, we already know this."

"Let her finish!" stated the Chief, as he cut his eyes sharply across the room. He turned back toward the young student, folded his hands on the desk, and smiled at her.

"Please continue, Miss," he said.

"Mr. President, if the two cyclonic systems were to be at the exact same wind speeds and pressure levels, they could possibly meld into one. This storm could have a cataclysmic affect!"

The silence was deafening in the room.

"So what exactly are the odds of this happening?" inquired the leader.

One of the scientists answered, "Why, it could be a billion to one, or more, Sir."

The Army Chief of Staff spoke out, "This discussion is preposterous! I suggest we adjourn this circus, and let's all go have some well-deserved breakfast."

A few of the assembly began nodding in agreement and shuffling their feet, like they were about to be dismissed.

"Just how strong could it be, this 'imaginary storm'?" Asked the President.

The young student responded, "Sir, my models conclude that the systems' strength would double at the very least, and may even exponentiate after that."

The President stood up and instructed the others, "Monitor the storm until zero 900 hours. If the models coincide any further, we shall declare a National State of Emergency, Implement Def Con 3 status, and order a mass evacuation of the entire Eastern seaboard. Prepare for a category eight hurricane."

"But Sir, there is no such thing as a category eight hurricane!" he heard one say.

"There is now," responded the President. "That is all, Gentlemen."

The Commander in Chief turned to the attentive stenographer, stating, "Thank you for your time, Ms. Turner."

"My pleasure, Mr. President," she responded, "but you can call me Paige."

The force of the conjoined storms intensified. The impending force of the storm of all creation had manifested. Armageddon was near for all that lay in its path. The evacuation procedures had evolved into a mass panic, as the largest human exodus ever recorded fled the eastern seaboard of the United States. The President was at a loss for what to do next, as the entourage of officials were summoned to reconvene once more. The assemblage began filing into the West Wing corridor, passing by the astute marine guard.

"Mr. President, we have a possible solution." stated the Admiral, "If we were to deposit a nuclear device into the eye of the storm, upon detonation, our theory of probability states that the blast will disperse it entirely."

"Sir, I beg to differ!" shouted the astrophysics scholar. "Dispersing a natural atmospheric occurrence of this scale could result in mass changes to the air currents around the globe, more than likely diverting the jet stream. The repercussion possibilities could be devastating to the planet. We might even blow a hole in the ozone!" he pleaded, as his hands gestured upwards.

"Nonsense," decreed the Defense Secretary, "This isn't a science fiction novel!"

The stenographer raised her eyebrow as if she had just got caught.

The President intervened, "Gentlemen, how many people will die if we do nothing?"

The room was silent.

"Initiate Def Con 1 status," he stated boldly, "and may God help us all."

As he turned away, the Commander in Chief paused; His index finger pointing upward, as if in contemplation of his next comment.

"How shall we deliver the weapon?" he asked.

"Sir, our ballistic missile capabilities are the envy of the world." stated the air commander, "There is little concern in this regard."

The President asked, "What about the Enola Gay?"

The collective consortium erupted in disbelief at what they had just heard.

"This is ridiculous!" stated one respondent, "A World War Two era Bomber?"

The Vice Admiral stepped forward. "Sir, with all respect, what are you proposing, and why?"

The young intern fought back an intuitive smile, as the leader of the free world clasped his hands behind his back.

"Gentlemen, on August 6, 1945, an American B-29 Superfortress delivered a weapon that killed tens of thousands of our fellow human beings. Perhaps now, the same machine can be used to save lives, rather than take them."

The Brigadier General scoffed,

"Sir, as interesting as this scenario sounds, there are only a handful of those aircraft in existence today."

The Admiral of the Navy interjected, "He is correct, Sir. The remaining ones are merely display pieces in museums."
The Air Force Commander spoke laughingly, "Besides, who would we get to fly it? Our pilots would be lost without a computer screen in the cockpit!"

The Commander in Chief offered no response, holding back instead like a card dealer awaiting the first bet. The silence was broken, as the Marine guard snapped into a full salute.

"Permission to speak, Sir" he asked. All eyes in the room focused on the unlikely inquisitor.

"Go ahead, son," answered the Head of State.

"There is one, Sir. My great grandfather flew a B-29 over Normandy, Sir."

A member of the group commented, "That's commendable, Son, but even if he were still capable, we don't have one of those bombers."

"That's what I mean, Sir." responded the Marine, "He has one on his farm in Kansas, in a hangar behind the corn silo."

There was a clicking sound. A doorknob turned.

"Sir, the press corps has assembled in the Rose Garden," said the staff informant.

"If you will excuse me, gentlemen, I must report to the people," stated the President, as he straightened his tie. As he left the room, he turned back toward them. "One more thing; you better top off the gas tanks and check the oil, because the whole world will be watching."

Operation Eagles Redemption, October 1, 2025

At approximately 0400 hours, the Boeing B-29 Bomber lifted off from Tyndall Air Force Base in North Florida, followed by Two F22 Raptors as escorts. The seasoned veterans piloted the iconic Super-fortress toward the East coast, maintaining a heading into the eye of the massive storm.

As the aged aircraft flew high above the cyclonic formation, the veteran pilot announced, "Boys, hang on to your briefs! We're about to dive."

The skilled aviator pushed the joystick forward, while pulling back on the cabled throttle. As the winged fuselage dove toward the center of the storms rotation, the crew leader announced, "Set coordinates, Fellas, we only have one bullet."

"Prepare to release ordnance," ordered the second in command. "Whadd'ya got, Gunny?"

"Target in sight and locked on, Sir," reported the navigator.

"It's now or never boys!" announced the Captain, "On Three.... One,... Three!"

"Release!" shouted the co-pilot.

The 90-year-old Colonel pulled back on the stick, while snatching the throttle wide open. The four eighteen-cylinder supercharged power plants engaged at full torque, pressing the occupants back into their seats, as the vintage propellers pulled the resurrected aircraft up and out of the atmospheric abyss.

"Woo-hoo! It's time to Skee-daddle!" hollered the World War 2 veteran. The accompanying raptors took their place on each side of the fleeing bomber, as they soared high and away from the drop zone.

"That wasn't funny Cappy!" said the second officer, "One, three?

Not funny at all."

Upon detonation, the 20 megaton warhead sent shock waves across the equator. Seismic readings were picked up as far as Tokyo and Manila, as the mushroom cloud began to unfurl. The world held its breath, and time seemed to stand still.

BEAUTIFUL WORLD

    I drove in from work yesterday, tired, irritated, and downright angry at everything around me. I pulled off the highway, past the parking lot, and turned off my truck. I rolled down the window, while glancing out at the ocean. It was just after sunset, the skies and the oceans still illuminated.

    I saw the silhouette of a large pelican floating slightly offshore, with her two young offspring around her. Right above, a flock of seagulls flew over them, heading their way into the horizon. I took a double take, thinking to myself just how beautiful it was, when a pod of bottle nose dolphins crested the waves right in the middle of the scene.

    Suddenly, everything I was upset or stressed about disappeared. I felt as if my petty little self-invented problems meant nothing. It is a beautiful world; all we have to do is notice it.

CAPTAIN DAVEY

The cowardly attacker raised his club above the trapped pup in a gesture for the killing blow. As the piece of tree limb began its quick descent toward its intended victim, the momentum was abruptly stopped. The mischievous young boy looked up to see the fist of a large man holding the other end of the wooden weapon.

"That's a fine grip you got there, Ladd!" stated the impromptu intervener.

"But now I have the other end of it. How strong a feller are ya?"

The boy was quickly out-wrestled, as the sea captain erupted in a chuckling laughter, directing the wooden object onto the posterior of the young antagonist.

The Captain thought, 'There is an evil inside of this one."

The Errant boy turned back toward his punisher, screaming, "My father will hear of this!"

"Aahh Ladd, I'll make sure of it," replied the scolding seafarer. …"and I might just smack his buttocks as well, for not raisin' ya right! Now go home, Lucious Von Progue, while you can still walk!"

The seasoned sailor bent over, and gently picked up the cowering puppy.

Ten Years Later….

"Look at 'em, scurrying along like jackals," he thought, as he tossed the braided sisal loop off the port bow, securing the cleat.

"No fittin' man would let his boys be such as this," he muttered.

The large wooden hull came to rest against the harbor piles.

"You there! What is your name?" he demanded. The young boy stopped in his tracks, as if to be caught in an act of mischief.

"D-david, sir," he stuttered, "M-my name is David."

A simple nod from the inquisitor sufficed in calming the boy's nature.

"Well, around here, your name is Davey," announced the Captain, "Be warned, you'll get no free meals on this deck, Ladd!"

The young wayfarer looked down at the splintered plank, the only avenue between the docks ledge and the decks edge. The young explorer wasted no time boarding the vessel, his two blue eyes staring all around in awe of the masted schooner, its sails furled, its ropes properly tended.

"Is that your dog, Sir?" asked the boy.

"Why, if you mean Bongo, I might tempt me-self to thinkin' I was his human instead," boasted the tender.

The young visitor, a mere ten years of age, more or less, was somewhat of a ragamuffin; his sandy blonde hair unkempt, his clothing tattered.

"Where are your parents, boy?" asked the bearded sailor. "Do they know where you are?"

The child responded; "I never knew my father, Sir. However my Mum speaks highly of him."

The attentive shepherd trotted over to the youth, sat back on his haunches, and raised his paw.

"Why, he wants to shake hands!" said the boy gleefully, while reaching out to accept the offer.

"Nice to meet you, Mr. Bongo!"

The Captain nodded, stating, "Why, Mr. Bongo here is the finest shipmate to ever sail the high seas!"

"Now, you might best be running along now, Ladd… Bongo and I must prepare to set sail."

The pilot and his pup turned toward the galley scuttle.

"But, please, Sir," shouted the waif, "Can you teach me how to tie knots? I-I've always wanted to know how to tie knots…"

For the next few hours the salty sea captain and his accidental apprentice tied knots, swabbed decks, and tended sails, while the seasoned instructor told stories of his life upon the sea.

The boy returns daily, and every afternoon, he states that he must return to his mum, on time. The captain routinely retires to his quarters; and writes in his diary. As time passes, the Captain questions the child's welfare, until one day, he decides to follow him home, unnoticed. He finds the boy sleeping alone under a trestle; his mother missing for years; kidnapped by pirates while unloading a merchant vessel.

⊷⊶

'Twas midnight when the salty sailor sequestered himself to his quarters. Once again opening his diary, taking his quill in hand, the author stared blindly through the lamplight, then began to write.

"Oh my sweetest Madeline, has it been ten years? I wish I knew where you were, why did you leave? I love you so, and pray that one day the fortunes of time shall grant me the joy of once again taking
you into my arms. I am not a learned man of poetry, yet these words encompass my thoughts when your memory enters my mind..."

>   Through mine eyes,
>   Looking through the blue
>   I often think of you
>   And where you are...
>   Through our eyes
>   We saw the world our way
>   Although you did not stay
>   You're in my heart..."

The Captain placed the feathered pen back into its well, while gently blowing on the page, drying the fresh ink. He then closed the worn ledger, extinguished the flame from his lamp, and drifted off to sleep.

∽∾

"Permission to speak freely, sir," asked the boy.
"Carry on," replied the Captain.
"How do the two of you navigate a ship as large as this? Just one man and one shepherd, piloting a great sailing vessel?"
His instructor responded, "Why Ladd, it's a combination of levers, pulleys, gadgets and gears.!"
His canine quartermaster's ears perked up.
"Oh yes, and you have to have Bongo here, as your deckhand!" he chuckled gleefully. The grateful owner reached down, ruffling the pup's fur all about his neck.
"Bongo-boy, raise the main-sail," he instructed.

The four-legged first mate trotted over to a large sisal loop hanging off of a wooden deck-peg. Young Davey watched in awe, as the highly trained shepherd took the rope into his jaws, pulling it across the roller pulley; the counterweights assisting in hoisting the large canvas sail to the long arm. He then secured it onto the wooden gear cleat.

"This is a fine schooner, Ladd. She hosts six cannons," boasted the sailor.

The shepherd's ears perked, at the recognition of the command word. The captain belted out a hearty laugh, stating, "And Bongo, here, why he is in charge of every one!"

⋧⋦

Every evening, when the last lamps have gone out, she carves. After being the slave servant for years to the pirate captain and his crew, her weary hands propel her mind elsewhere, to freedom one day, perhaps. But for now, the piece of cork and odd matchsticks will have to do. She pulls out a few rags she has collected, and a little ball of sewing thread. As the nights go on, her therapeutic masterpiece takes shape. Whilst upon this particular evening, the model is complete. The apprehended artist inserts the tiny replica into the blown bottle, and seals it with a cork.

The cabin door abruptly opens, the challenging abuser demanding, "What are you doing?"

"Just a hobby," she trembled.

The furious despot lashed out, the tearful maiden cowering back in fear.

"Your hobby is tending to my crew! Now forget this drivel, and get back to work!" he ordered.

The drunken pirate grabbed the bottle, aggressively hurling it up through the galley scuttle. The desperate hostage watched, as her creation landed on the top deck.

The glass cylinder began rolling around the upper level, responding to the pitch of the seas; the scandalous crew taking note. One by one, the pirates gathered around the glazed object. A game of sorts erupted, as the object's creator witnessed the dirty deck mates taking turn kicking the rolling target. Von Progue fumed his way back toward his cabin, puffing like an ill-lit cannon.

"Here's one to ye, Cappy!" boasted one player, as he lobbed the glass capsule into his leader's path.

Laughter erupted, as the leader of the ship of thieves volleyed the misconceived puck through an opening in the ships top rail.

The maiden began to weep, as the men slowly walked away.

Once the bullying assembly had disbanded, the maiden looked up into the moonlight. She smiled softly, as she watched her little bottle of clues gently drift away with the currents.

The Captain strolled past the various fishing vessels to the gangplank that led up to the admiral's ship.

"Admiral Driggers, it's good to see you well, Sir."

"Likewise, Captain, what brings you here?" responded the officer.

"I am seeking information on a woman that may have been kidnapped by pirates, from this very harbor, Sir." he answered.

"Follow me to my quarters." the admiral stated, "There is something I want to show you"

The two entered the ship's office, the admiral retrieving two small glasses from a cabinet, along with a flask of brandy.

The senior commander opened a wooden trunk at the base of his bunk, and removed an item wrapped in sailcloth, placing it upon his desk.

As he peeled back the layers, he stated, "This was found washed up on the beach a fortnight ago; and it appears to be an exact replica of Von Progue's ship." After close examination of the artifact, the two former shipmates proposed a toast, then parted ways, determined to rescue the maiden and purge the seas of the wretched scum that could proliferate such an injustice upon it.

The captain strolled down the gangplank, with the cloaked artifact tucked under his arm.

"Good day, gentlemen," he spoke, as he passed the two sentries.

The young apprentice lit an oil lamp, curled up into his bunk, and began flipping through the pages. The midnight hour was near, and the masted schooner was well away on its voyage.

The mighty wooden vessel rolled gently along in its buoyancy on the seas, its rhythmic movements constant; as perpetual as the tides on which it rode.

The Captain Had long since retired to his quarters, while Young Davey read aloud from the aging almanac, his canine shipmate watching attentively, as if to imply an understanding of the commentary.

"Bongo! We must inform the Captain!" declared the youth.

The duo sprang from their berth, quickly ascending to the main deck. The night skies had faded; the light of a new day was upon the horizon.

The slumbering wayfarer was unaware of the concerned interveners, as he heard, "Captain! Come quick!"

The words were followed by a loud knock on the door, then another, the young squire reporting, "Captain! You must rise immediately, Sir! There appears to be a big thunderstorm approaching, Sir! "

The trio raced out onto the top deck, the captain looking out onto the horizon.

"That's no thunderstorm, Ladd!" exclaimed the lead sailor, adding,
"Bongo, open the loading hatch. Prepare to lower the cannons."

The trio quickly went to work securing the vessel, then retreated into a lower section of the ship.

"Take these ropes, and tether yourself off tight!" instructed the navigator, "This is going to be a rough ride."

The trio held steadfast, bunkered in the security of the chartroom.
As the massive hurricane quickly approached, the wooden vessel was tossed like a corked bottle; yet the hatches held firmly. The tightly tethered masts shook violently in the cyclonic winds, as the masterfully joined planks that lined the hull groaned loudly through the tempests fury.

The high seas subsided, and the three shaken shipmates slowly emerged through the galley scuttle.

"Thank God, it's over," panted the boy, as the captain began to assess the situation. The nautical nemesis slowly glanced around in a panoramic observation. The darkness surrounded their little spot of calm.

"It's not over, Ladd," regretted the Captain, "for we have quite another dilemma now. You see, now, we reside in its eye."

The steadfast schooner continued to creak and groan, the young apprentice reporting, "We're taking on water, Sir."

"We won't survive another bout with this storm, Ladd," responded the worried mariner. The captain peered into the blackness of the tempest, the massive system moving around them.

He turned to the young boy and his faithful dog, then glanced across the deck of his ship. Feeling a sense of impending doom, the senior helmsman was at a loss as to what to do next. The wrinkles on his weathered face became taught, as he looked up through the eye of the massive hurricane.

"Is this to be our fate, Lord?" he shouted, "Have you brought us this far, only to have us sucked into the abyss?"

The weary navigator then dropped to his knees, as Davey and Bongo looked on. Bowing his head, he began to pray....

"I beg thee, Lord, take me if you wish, but please spare the boy, and let Bongo be safe with him."

Suddenly, he felt a warmth cloaking his face, and as he opened his eyes, he looked up to see a single ray of sunlight piercing through the center of the eye wall. The beam of light crossed the deck toward the bow, then travelled over the waves to the edge of the blackness, where it quickly disappeared to the northeast. The captain's face relaxed as he felt a swelling of hope enter his soul.

"Drop the sails!" he said in an instant. "We shall take to the helm, use the winds to our backs, and sail our way out of this hell!"

The ship was in full sail, as it approached the edge of the eye wall. The ship followed a circular pattern with the storm, and as it approached the darkness, the winds filled the sails. The captain held onto the ship's wheel with all the strength he could muster.

"Hold on Lads! We only have one shot at this!" he announced. In a calculated maneuver, the master navigator aimed the large vessel in the exact direction of the wind, and the masted schooner shot through to the outer edge of the hurricanes rotation.

"Whoo hoo!!" exclaimed Davey, as the great vessel became airborne, skipping along the massive waves like a pebble on a lake.

◈◈

The Schooner moored into the safety of a tiny inlet, hidden from view by the vessels that lay in the harbor on the other side of the dunes. The Eve of the Noel was upon the earth. The midnight sky was eerily clear; the moon, bright.

Davey the apprentice and Bongo the ship dog lowered the nets, while the Captain lowered the anchor. The three shipmates prepared to go ashore, and as they lowered their skiff into the murky waters of the lagoon, the Captain whispered, "Act normal Lads, for I assure you we are being watched."

The bow of the skiff scrubbed the shore, and the three adventurists disembarked, making their way through the underbrush, then up to the top of the sand dune. Through the clearing, they could see the lights from the small village below...

"There it is," stated the Captain, "the tavern of Thieves and Bastards. Now, try to blend in."

They quietly made their way to edge of a side street. The saloon was in full swing, the gas lamps ablaze, the ale flowing freely.

Young Davey faded into the shadows, then emerged holding a barmaids mop, meandering through the pub like a busboy.

The Captain approached the tender of the barrels.

The saloon keeper was none other than a man by the name of Scoggins; A purveyor of piscatorial preparations sure to please the pickiest of palates; A part time harbormaster, and full- time imbiber, yet went by the name of "Killer", as to keep his piratious patrons at bay...

"What's your pleasure, traveler?" he asked.

The Captain responded, "I'll have a pint of your stoutest, and anything you know about a kidnapped woman."

The attendant pulled the tap lever open, filling the earthen mug to the top, its sudsy foam overflowing.

"Tis one thing to play with a snake, quite another to let it bite you," the tender offered, as he handed away the urn.

"I only kill the venomous ones," stated the thirsty patron.

Suddenly, the Senior sailor felt a nudge into his lower back; He knew all too well what the barrel of a flintlock felt like.

"What do you want?" asked the Captain, as he slowly raised his hands.

"Give us the diary," spoke a crumbling voice.

The threatened saloon patron raised his hands slightly higher, as if to be in surrender. The murderous challenger was unaware that the gestures made by his would-be victim were signals;

Bongo the shepherd instantly focused on the mugger. There was a second nudge from the end of the cast barrel.

"A seeker of the treasure, are ya?" inquired the offended adventurer, "Well, if you treasure that arm of yours, ye might be well suited to lowering that pistol," he continued.

"I'll do no such thing," snarled the pirate, "Now, hand over the diary, or I'll spark yer belly full of lead faster than ya can blink."

The Captain stood fast, while slowly placing his thumb to his middle finger; an unnoticed gesture in the assailant's eyes.

The Captain stated, "I'll offer ye one more chance, Ladd. Surrender your weapon,"

His offender responded, "And it is you, who are out of chances," as he cocked his pistol.

The clicking sound of the muskets hammer was instantly followed by the snap of the captain's fingers, as Bongo the shepherd leaped like a flash, taking the perpetrators forearm into his jaws, sinking his fangs deep. The robber collapsed, screaming in pain, as the captain turned to take the pistol for his own.

All eyes in the saloon turned to focus on the surprise altercation, as the winner of the bout began interrogating his would-be attacker.

"Where is the woman? Who is holding her hostage?" inquired the senior helmsman.

The defeated mugger looked around the pub; while commenting loudly, "I will tell you nothing!" followed by a painful whisper, "They will kill me if I do."

"Fair enough," responded his questioner, "Bongo, take the gentleman outside." The loyal shepherd maintained his vise-like grip, leading the arrestee out of the tavern, and into the back alley.

"Please make him let go!" begged the tearful hostage; the pain almost unbearable.

"Answer my questions now, for Bongo is growing impatient," was the response.

The Captain raised his hand again, placing his middle finger to his thumb. The captive criminal's eyes opened wide, as he exclaimed, "His name is Von Progue!"

The aggressive interviewer nodded, inquiring, "Where is his ship?"

The suffering respondent replied: "Around the bend of the harbor. To the east lies a slough."

Young Davey continued to play his role, and swabbed the puddles of spilled ale, the stench almost as obnoxious as the drunken pirates that wallowed in it.

"Do you sail on a pirate ship?" the boy asked one of the patrons.

"Indeed I do, and what is it of your business, Boy?" he answered.

"Sir, I've always wanted to sail on a Pirate ship. Can I sail with you, please? I will work for free."

The villainous banter abounded about the bar, yet was quickly subdued, as the tavern keeper took a steel ladle, repeatedly striking the side of the large brass spittoon that lay at the edge of the tenders table, signaling closing time. One by one, the inebriated patrons began staggering out of the ale-house and into the streets.

"Come with me, Boy," stated the drunken pirate; "I'll show you the way to the ship."

❧❧

The captain's apprentice boarded the pirate's ship, unbeknownst to the crew as to his identity. He was instructed to take a bunk at the stern of the armory deck.

"Thank you, Sir," offered the boy. "Might I have some water, please? I'm awfully thirsty, Sir."

The drunken crewmember belched, "Walk the planks past the cannons, the barrels of water lie in the bow. Now scurry off with ye!"

Young Davey waited by his bunk, until all lamps had extinguished for the night. He quietly strolled past the huge iron guns, to the oaken caskets that lie just beyond. He then carefully removed a bladder flask from his breeches, and filled it, filling then another, while placing them back onto his belt-loop. One by one, the unlikely spy pulled the wicks out of each cannon, filling the powder chambers with water.

❦

   The night sky began to lighten into a soft blue, the dawn breaking the horizon; a new day was at hand. The captain navigated the schooner around the bend, and into the inlet of the secluded slough. The approaching schooner outflanked the outlaw vessel, as the evil pirate leader ordered, "Prepare to fire!"
   One by one, the scallywag crew lit their fuses, the flames dying quickly into the wet gunpowder that lie in the breeches.
   "Nice try, Boys! But how's this for a volley?" chuckled the Captain, as he lit a fuse of his own. The bang was deafening, as the eighty-pound Iron ball shot out from its bore, arcing across in a calculated trajectory, severing the main mast of the kidnapper's ship. The wooden assemblage of ropes and canvasses gave way, pulling the mizzen and aft poles down as well.
   The infamous pirate's ship lay still in the water, as the captain scrolled over to his second cannon; torch in hand.
   Von Prague was quick to respond defiantly, "You are but one, Captain; surely you cannot defeat my entire crew."
   "Well, Ladd, the next one's going straight through your hull," professed the senior helmsman, "How many of your crew wish to drown in a sinking vessel?"
   The pirate's entourage mingled and mumbled amongst each other, their mannerisms displaying a mutual sense of negativity toward the challenger's proposal.
   "Now, release the woman to me! I shall pivot my gangplank onto your foredeck. Have that young boy escort her."
   The leader of the pirates turned back toward his men, mumbling,
"The man is a fool! He simply cannot tend a cannon and lower a plank at the same time."
   The desperate villain took a musket, laying a bead on the captain; and awaited his opportunity. A puzzled look came over his face, as he saw the captain handing the torch to his attentive canine

shipmate. Bongo the shepherd trotted over to the massive iron gun, and paused, awaiting his next command.

"Lower the gun, Sir!"

The leader of the ship of thieves glanced up from his firing stance.

"Who said that?" he responded.

"It is I," stated one of the indentured crew. There was a grumbling brewing amongst the shipmates.

"I agree with him," added another, "Let him have the woman"

The rest of the scallywag crew surrounded their leader, as he quickly succumbed to their demands.

"Luscious! Go fetch the wench from my brig."

The two soon emerged from the entrance to the ship's deck quarters, the hostage maiden tethered by the wrists, a woven sack over her head.

As they approached the gangplank, the captain ordered, "Not him."

"Have another boy walk her across. That one, over there" he continued, as he casually waved his finger toward his undercover apprentice.

The hostage was escorted aboard the rescuing vessel, and was quickly sequestered into the captain's quarters. The captain raised his hands, placing his fore finger to his thumb once again.

"But you promised!" He heard from the villainous populace.

"Indeed, I did, lads! No sense in polluting the lagoon with this scow."

"Bongo, cannon three," he commanded. The protective pup trotted over to the third iron gun, and placed the torches flame to the wick.

The blast was deafening, as the well-aimed projectile found its mark, destroying the large wooden rudder from the rear of the enemy ship.

"Float along fellows, I'll send a rescue."

"Davey! Full to port!"

With the confident student at the helm, and the winds filling the sails, the trio turned toward the mouth of the slough, and into the open waters of the gulf. At the entrance to the secluded waterway, lay another majestic vessel.

"Admiral Driggers! Always a pleasure, Sir!" the Captain exclaimed, "I trust that you will dispense of these various vagabonds accordingly."

"As well with you, Captain David! We will take it from here."

The young boy looked over at his mentor, thinking, "Captain David..?"

The sun was beginning to set, as the well-tended schooner navigated toward the west, sailing away from the scourge of its past. Darkness fell, and the victorious sailors entered into a tiny inlet, dropping their anchor.

"Come along, ladds! We must tend to the maiden," instructed the Captain. The three compatriots slowly opened the door to the captain's quarters.

"Why, there's no one here," feared the boy.

They glanced over to the door leading into the chartroom.
"Miss, are you in there?"

The door opened, as the emancipated prisoner stepped out into view. The captain froze in disbelief, his face turning pale, and seemingly all at once, they spoke out loudly,

"Madeline! My God, is it you?"

"David?"

"Mother!"

"David!"

"Madeline!"

The captain and the kid turned, looking perplexed at one another.

"Yes, you are his father," she spoke, as she ran to greet her long lost love.

The three lost souls had finally found each other, engaging into a loving embrace, as the calm seas gently rocked the masted schooner.

Suddenly, there was a loud blast from the second cannon, the trail of gunpowder illuminating the starry sky like a celebratory firework. The reunited family ran out to the top deck, as they watched Bongo the shepherd lighting the remaining cannons, one by one.

October 11, 2018

It was then that I awoke from my dream-ridden slumber, quite an entertaining distraction from the reality that I was to face today. The reality that just yesterday, a category 5 hurricane had come from seemingly nowhere, and inflicted a direct hit over my hometown; destroying the little motel on the beach, and everything else in its path.

My mind was in a daze, my thoughts convoluted; "there's just too much to think about," I pondered, as I drove out of the parking lot of the budget inn. I remembered how I had watched the storms track on the weather radar the day before, and how I had sat stunned and speechless on the end of that motel room bed…I was not sure what lay before me, but I knew I had to get back to Mexico Beach as fast as I could. I had to go help the others. Just then, the phone rang.

"Mr. Kent; this is the Mexico Beach Police Department" the caller stated. "We regret to inform you that your property has been completely destroyed by hurricane Michael…"

"Thank you," I responded, as I began to hang up the phone.

"Mr. Kent..." "There's something else"...I heard...

"Hello?"… "Yes, Officer, what do you mean?"…

The words I heard then shocked me;

my cell phone falling into the floorboard.

I raced back to the little beach, and ran to the spot
where the small motel had sat snuggly in the sand;
only to find the building gone, its floors reduced into rubble.

I stood speechless in a sense of amazed wonderment;
as I looked up at the spectacle of the masts, the curved planks, The centuries old craftsmanship; The decaying relic of another time resurrected by a random notion of nature.

The category five super storm had miraculously washed
up the seventeenth century masted schooner, placing her gently upon the dunes in place of the little motel,

Her bow facing defiantly away from the sea…

205

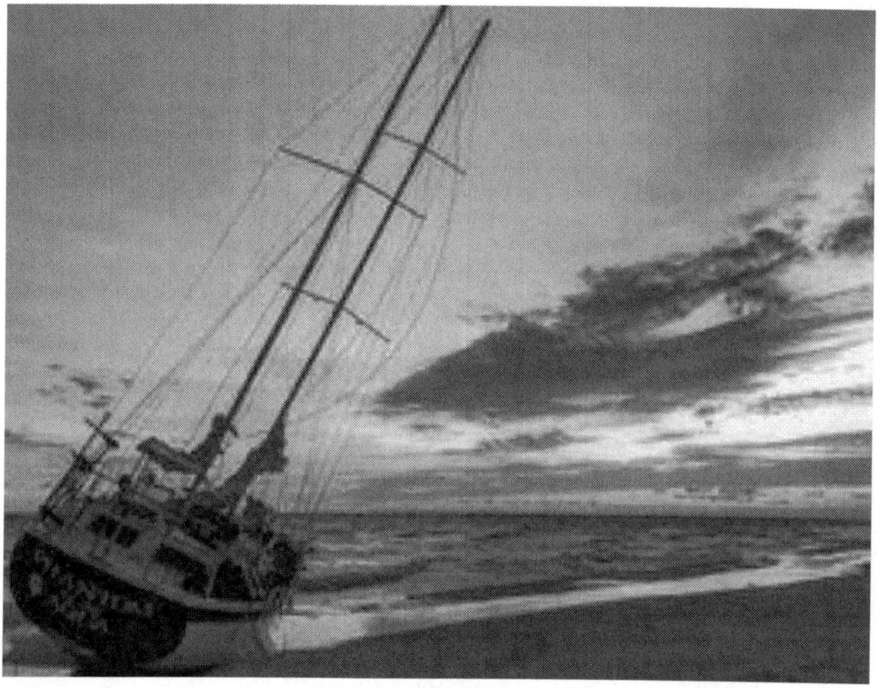

THE PHANTOM OF THE AQUA

The storm of storms had made landfall. The skies became darker, as the winds and rain persisted into the evening hours…. The young couple had ridden out the storm in the little beach house, the power failing hours prior; the lightning illuminating their world from blackness like an erratic strobe light.

There was a hurried knock from outside, then another, then again, each one slightly louder and more quickly paced than its predecessor.
The beam from her flashlight cut through the darkness; then danced around the room as she made her way toward the door.

At the entrance to the bungalow stood a frail old man, soaking wet, his face weathered and weary, his hair white and colorless, his clothes ragged.

"Please, you must come help," he begged, "My vessel…it has run aground. Please hurry; the girl is in grave danger."

The young woman turned back toward her approaching husband.

"Honey, there is a gentleman here who needs help," she informed him. Suddenly, a large bolt of lightning struck the horizon. Its thunderous report was deafening; it's light blinding.

The despondent visitor vanished instantly.

"Who is it, dear?" Her partner inquired.

"I don't know," She responded, "I thought I saw someone…"

Later that evening, the old man returned to the woman in a dream, pleading for help in saving the young girl's life. In her sleep, she sees hazy, surreal images of a serial rapist and murderer; a young girl held captive; a listing curvature of planks illuminated by fading oil lamps;
A perverted demon enslaving its prey inside a stranded hijacked vessel, while waiting for the high tide.

The woman woke up in muffled screaming, as if she is bound and gagged herself.

"He was back, the man who needed help," she told her husband.

Her compassionate bedmate held her in tight embrace, offering comfort from the fear of her subliminal encounter.

Daylight returned once more to the little bungalow, the dawn of a new day in stark contrast to the events of the day before. The young couple began to get busy, cleaning up the effects of yesterdays' weather, and checking the cabin for damage.

"I found this old typewriter in the attic", announced her husband, as he clamored down the wooden staircase that led up to a storage area above. "It thought you might want to tinker with it until the power comes back on."

She opened the frayed, fabric covered case, and looked down at the familiar contraption with a child-like wonderment.

"Tak...Tak," she heard, as her fingers applied pressure to the keys.

"What a familiar sound," She thought, remembering it from her childhood, when her mother was a typist.

She looked over the dusty relic with an unexplainable passion, gently turning the drum, feeling the interplaying increments of detents, and wondering what it must have been like to write on an instrument such as this, as so many others had in the past.

The keys proved somewhat fluid, as much as a counterbalance could allow; the ribbon dry. She turned the spool in search of a damper source of ink.

"Meeooww" she heard, as the resident kitten-cat stepped up onto the keys,

"Tak...Tak..."She directed the cat off the keyboard and onto a path toward the kitchen. There was a knock at the door. After a few words were spoken and formalities exchanged, her feline companion was shuttled off to the veterinarian.

Later that evening, her attention turned once again to the antiquated implement. She worked methodically, carefully wrapping the loose ribbon around the reel, threading it between the clasps, and across the drum to the other side hosting the return bar.

She continued to turn the spool, eventually finding a section of fresh ribbon.

"How intriguing!" she thought, as she pressed a key.
"H"

It worked! The little hammer made its mark, through the ink-laden strip, and onto the aging, yellowed paper.

She continued, "e, l, l, o," each key performing efficiently.

The midnight sky was upon her, and soon the young couple would prepare themselves for bed. Sleep arrived quickly, and as they drifted off into a state of unconscious slumber, her mind was busy inventing stories in which she might one day write about. As she delved into the abyss of the deepest of sleeps, she heard a sound; a sound that drew her back into the world of the wakened.

"Tak...Tak."

"Silly cat," she thought, as her mind drifted in and out of a hazy realm of consciousness.

"Tak...Tak...Tak."

The puzzled slumberer arose, only to remember that the cat was gone for the night. She froze still, glancing down at the old typewriter. Below her self-punched letters, were the words,

"Please, you must send help...The girl is in grave danger."

A bolt of fear ran through her, her hands trembling, as she motioned them toward the keys. Tak...Tak...Tak.." sounded the key hammers, her lips forming the words in whispers, as her fingers transferred her thoughts onto the page.

"Who are you?" She asked, followed by, "How do we find her?"... "Where is the girl?"
She stood silently in the darkness, for what seemed like an eternity, her eyes becoming heavy once again with sleepiness.

"I must be dreaming," she thought, as she turned away from the vintage apparatus, eagerly anticipating her return to the solace of the feather bed that lay just beyond the doorway.
"Tak...Tak...Tak..." The sounds pierced the silence of the night, as random keys took turns depressing downward on their own. The robed respondent turned back in awe, watching carefully as each hammer left its cradle and struck the ink-fortified cloth, leaving its imprint on the cellulotic substrate... As the key marks formed words, she followed along, reading them aloud...

"I am the captain- of the high jacked merchant vessel "*Aqua.*"

The keys then lay still, as her mind attempted to reason with the meaning of the response. She noticed that the typeset had run out of room on the cylindrical drum, so she instinctively reached for the return bar, and gently flexed the handle, sending the carriage back into its prior position. Letter by letter, the supernatural scripting continued, until the message was complete.

"Stranded... on a secluded dune; - among large fronds,

"Where the East meets the West;"...

"Where the ocean meets the river, and time is - uncertain."

"Now please hurry...The girl may perish by a fortnight."

The high tides arrive; soon the floundering vessel will right itself, taking to the seas once more.

The blast from the air horn was deafening, as the Coast Guard cutter overtook the slow moving coal barge, ultimately passing the floating behemoth on its port side, while navigating the intra-coastal avenue to the mouth of the bay. There ahead lie the bridge that symbolically separated the time zones observed by the local residents. The twin engine watercraft propelled itself between the bridges support piers and out into the open waters of the channel leading to the sea, toward the lone island known for its' dense population of palms.
"That must be it", announced the pilot, as he pointed at the towering display of foliage circling the modest atoll.
The shaken hostage is quickly located and transported to safety on board the rescue boat, as others patrolled the adjacent shorelines and sloughs in an unsuccessful search for the kidnapper.

The vessel narrowly escapes capture, as the errant operator quickly tends to the sails, filling them with a strong Northeastern wind. The oceans rise, as the previously welcomed winds strengthen into gale force, shearing the sails from their masts and leaving the piratious perpetrator adrift on the high seas.

The wayward fugitive drifts for days, then weeks, consumed by the fear of being captured by the authorities. As the waves toss the hull violently, the sinister sailor tethers himself to the main mast. He begins to become delusional, as hunger and thirst begin to overtake him.

Darkness consumed the sky once more, the phosphorescence from the waves offering the only light on the surreal surroundings. The darkness of the infinite sky melded in with the blackness of the aquatic abyss, offering the fugitive a sense of weightlessness, as if he was being held in a suspension of time and space... A bolt of fear shoots through him, as he turns to see the ghost of the captain standing at the helm.

A mere wisp of a vision, then again, a second look. The swirling winds and sea mist dispersing the likeness momentarily, only for the fog to regroup and again take on the form of the captain.

"Who are you? What are you?" gasped the dying escapee.

The captain's image materialized further, as the ghostly image began to speak.

"What be it then, this thing we call 'fate'?" inquired the apparition.

"Such a supposition on your part, the thoughts of mortality;" "Do ye consider thine own? We all face it, yet it is ye that should most fear its arrival."

The translucent spirit came closer, as the debilitated castaway frantically loosened his ropes. The frightened fugitive stumbled helplessly across the deck, the waves tossing the stranded vessel in violent turmoil.

The ethereal vision continued its torment.

"Unbeknownst to one as blind as yourself, I am resident of this vessel, Von Prague".. "I saw what you did,… every bit of it." smirked the face in the fog.

"Quite the suiting destiny for one such as yourself;
A proctor of malfeasoned fortune; an actor set on deceit,"

The ghostly image continued,

"Tis convenient for me, to consider eternity, for I am already there… You, on the other hand, live in fear of it."

The spirit turned away from the frightened absconder, only to quickly revert to his close attention, the face in the fog coming within inches of the perpetrators cheek.

"And what mere mortal should not?" snarled the atmospheric illusion…

"The thought of facing the unknown is a fearful one, is it not? Now may you feel such as your victims."

The eyes of the specter grew larger as it lifted its head while placing it's forefinger to its cheek; as if to be contemplating the composition of his contemptuous commentary.

A sinister grin formed on the captain's face as he heartlessly chuckled,
"The strange thing about thirsting to death, you see,"…
"The parched palate, the chaffed lips… Thirst burns into a man's soul, slowly draining his life like a dimming light."

The spirits smile relaxed, as its face became devoid of all expression, and in a stern, authoritative tone, decreed,

"Tonight is your night to die, Von Prague!"

The despondent drifter lunged at the transcendental instigator, and in blind rage, stumbled toward the galley scuttle, his feet becoming entangled in the ropes. The would-be attacker lost balance, falling headfirst into the lower hold; the last sisal loop becoming taught around his neck.

The ropes seized, flailing the snared criminal upright;

A lifelong reign of terror had come to an end, as the lifeless body of Luscious Von Prague swung freely with the rhythm of the , waves.

The breaking dawn had begun to lighten the horizon as the likeness of the Captain dispersed; and the phantom of the vessel known as "The Aqua" slowly dissipated; eventually evaporating into nothingness into the morning air…..

BACK TO SCHOOL

Be proud of who you are ...You are the descendant of all of your ancestors, you are the one. The one alive at this moment; The shining star; The result of centuries of love and trust...It is you, and each one of us, to live this miracle that we call life, to embrace it, to live it, and most importantly, to love it......

    I have been so frustrated with my life lately; the uncertainty, the lack of control, the overall confusion, that I asked myself; ; "When were you actually happy?" "At what time in your life do you remember being the most content?" I reverted straight back to elementary school in my mind..."Ahh, memories" It was a magical time then...So this morning I decided to live again like that....I got out of bed when it was still dark, brushed my teeth, and got dressed. (No coffee by the way, I'm in elementary school.) I rushed out to my truck, (School Bus), to go face the day...I had a brown paper bag with a sandwich, potato chips, and fruit in if. I Arrived precisely on time to school, (work), and studied at it until 11.30...That was lunch time. I stopped, and spent thirty minutes or so eating my lunch, talking to my friends, and relaxing.
Then back to class... (It's called work when you are an adult)...right at three o'clock, Dave asked me if I wanted to work late.

  "Sorry!" I said, "I'll miss my bus!"...At three twenty, I boarded the bus, (my truck), headed straight home, and dropped myself off.

 I had to do my homework first, (pay some bills, write some contracts,) then I could play outside for a while. Thirty minutes before dark was bath time. (Hot shower)...I put on my P.J.'s and made the table for dinner. (I ate everything on my plate, as well). I then washed the dishes, which gained me the privilege to watch television until bedtime at 9:00 o'clock. I got up this morning and did it again.

Going to do it tomorrow too…

THE REALM OF THE HEAVENS

"Patricia?"
"Yes, my Lord."
"He's downstairs,"
"I'm not ready, my Lord..."
"You knew this day would come..."
"Yes, my Lord"...
  The clouds passed by her feet, her angelic strides creating gentle wisps of currents, casually dissipating the cumulus masses into memory. As the clear spectrum of light surrounding her peripheral vision began to develop into a soft shade of blue, she paused.
"Go forth, so you may return," echoed the deitious voice.
"Then it will be my faith that carries me back to the land of the earthen, not mine feet, dear lord." She responded.
"So be it child,
So be it." She heard.
She turned her head down, placing one hesitant foot in front of the other,
And through the translucent aura, her eyes began to discern a spherical object far, far below, a familiar, yet distant sight..
    She moved closer still, as the orb in her view began taking on a myriad of shapes and colors, defining boundaries where the earths met the oceans... the soft white clouds created wisps of their own, as they cloaked the frail planet in an atmosphere of protection.
    From the infinities of the never-ending void she knew as the universe of all creation, she stared over at the shadows of a thousand souls, bound for centuries in their spatial, yet buoyant non-existence. They floated aimlessly, yet contained, their faces drawn, their mouths agape, as if in an aqueous pool of hopelessness and uncertainty; Some souls recently introduced, others evidencing an appearance suggesting eons of waiting.

A lone voice pierced through the low moans emanating from the consortium of the lost.. "Patricia!"…The angelic observer turned toward the newest of the arrivals; a familiar face; a life-long memory from her tenure among the mortals.

"Let me in!" he begged.

She maintained her peaceful presence; a soft glow surrounding her.

"I can't do that"' she responded,

"For your time has come to answer to the creator; to await and face your final judgment."

Three soft beams of light then descended upon her, drawing her back into the realm of the heavens, while the lost soul began to drift off with the others, its panicked pleadings becoming softer and more distant, until they completely faded away into the cosmic abyss…..

AN UNLIKELY MINIMALIST

One day it was stumbled upon;
Washed upon a distant beach.
A simple glass bottle; sealed with a cork;
Tossed into the waves.
Through its glazed iridescence,
I could see a handwritten scroll.....
Who was it, the one who cast this flask?
Be it a survivor?
Be it another?
Be it a lost soul; who in destitute measure;
Scribed their legacy,
Then set it free, to be carried by the currents;
A drifting message; floating in a sea of eternity,
In hopes of one day being discovered?

"If you are reading this, you must have found my bottle. I hope it fared the voyage intact. Please keep it as yours; and may it serve you well.

I had travelled a long journey through my life thus far, always aspiring to succeed as I was taught that I should, coerced by my peers during my youth, and like so many others around me in my adult life.

Society, as I saw it, seemed indoctrinated into the notion that the more one accumulates, whether it be material possessions, money, fame, or stature, the richer they become. Life, for most, was a competition of numbers; a comparison of worth based upon money.

I set out like the rest, spending my precious days chasing wealth. My time was consumed, toiling daily for long hours; a slave to the economic machine. I would go into debt to buy a vehicle to work in, then work to pay for the vehicle.

I would borrow money to buy land that I would never own, then work more hours to pay back the debt and taxes. I would obligate further, in order to build an impressive structure, as to prove my stature among the others.

These tasks were met with success, but at a higher price than I could have imagined. My time was no more my own. My life belonged to the others.

The pursuit of wealth, as perceived, is a strong desire among us. Always living slightly above our means, never quite being content,
always wanting a little bit more. This led to acquiring a large estate of debt; finding myself trapped. A slave to obligation, I was a mere purveyor of monies, tasked with shuttling it to the various recipients.

Surely, my efforts would pay off one day. One day, the debts would be paid. One day, when I was older, I would have more money to buy more things.

Then came that one morning, like so many others, yet starkly different from the rest. I got out of bed as usual, made coffee, and checked the answering machine. If it were any other day, I would have already been visited by a guest or two, in need of extra towels and such.
But not this particular day.

There were no guests. There were no cars in the parking lot. There was no traffic on the highway, except for an occasional law enforcement vehicle. Two officers drove up, climbed the stairs to my office, and sternly advised me to evacuate.

I agreed with their judgment, placed some odd clothes in a bag, and drove out of town.

"Daggum weather channel," I thought. "Always exaggerating things."

I travelled northeast, until I was out of the storm's projected path, ultimately checking into a motel room.

Change came in a whirlwind, as I watched everything I thought was important for so long disintegrate on a television radar screen. The inn on the shore was the first to go. Its age defined its structural inadequacy, the building collapsing into the torrent of the storm surge, so quickly that the winds did not carry any debris away. My trusty pickup truck had been transported into the forest, landing on top of pieces of damaged homes, totally inundated and destroyed.

A few miles up the road, I had an old mobile home, which was destroyed as well, but there were some salvageable items inside. I spent the next few days going through them, storing the collectibles in a cargo trailer borrowed from a friend.

Then the thieves came; the looters; the heartless opportunists. They broke in to the locked storage space, stealing tools, the remaining collectibles, and some sacred items from my childhood. They knew not what the items meant to me. They had no need for them, just a desire to scavenge and to hoard, with no regard for the victims of their perpetrations.

The cargo trailer was ransacked; all that remained were broken fragments, and a chest of drawers containing my salvaged clothing. As I opened one of the drawers, I was startled by a large rat, which jumped out of his lair, leaving behind the chewed and urine stained rags that I used to wear.

I realized that no matter what had been taken from me, I was still alive. I could not save those things, but I could save myself.

I began giving away all that was left, asking the neighbors to come into the remnants of my home, and feel free to take any and everything they needed. I discovered that the less I had, the better I felt. As each item was removed, I felt the burden of trivial ownership lifted off of me, giving me a sense of freedom that I had never experienced. I drove around in the new truck, owned by the bank, dispersing the last remaining items from my past. I gathered the very last of my worldly possessions, the ones not even worthy of stealing, the plastic spatulas, the empty flashlights, the broken lamps, and drove to a donation center.

On the way, I thought about what a wise man once said, "He who is without possessions, is truly a free man."

I had tasted freedom, and I liked it. I dropped off the rest of the items and drove away. My mind took me back in time, to a memory from 1982, still as fresh as it was the day that it happened.

There was a phone call.

"I'm on the way." I responded.

I stood alone, gazing through the plate glass window. There must have been noises from the footsteps in the corridor, or the sounds of the little metal wheels grumbling by, but I heard nothing. All of my senses focused on the frail little body lying behind the glass.

A voice broke through the barrier of my deepest thoughts.

"I see he has his father's receding hairline."

"Hello, doctor,' I responded, "Is he any better today?"

My son was a mere 18 months into this world, and for reasons unknown, had become unable to breathe. His tiny trachea had swollen; his only source of oxygen deprived. A plastic tube had been inserted into his mouth, extending into his lungs, in a desperate attempt to save his life. Our tear-filled eyes focused on each other, as I saw a tiny soul asking for none other than to be able to live.

I remember how helpless I felt, and how I questioned God's intentions back then.

My mind regained focus onto the present, while I pulled into a grocery store.

That is where I bought this bottle. It was a nice chardonnay, and I wanted to celebrate finally achieving my goal to own nothing; to be obligated to nothing; to be as free as a fish in the sea, or a bird in the sky.

The self-checkout alarm beeped, "Attendant needed for alcohol purchase." A smocked lady walked up and scanned her badge; the laser beam conferring with the computerized system. I walked out of the store, wine in hand.

At the entrance was a breezeway, with benches alongside. On the far end sat an elderly woman, holding a small aging dog. She was weeping silently, as I sat down beside her.

"What is wrong? Do you need help?" I quietly asked. She looked startled at first, but then began to confide in me. I learned that her money had been stolen, and she could not buy groceries for her grandchildren. I walked back into the store to the teller machine, and checked my account balance.

"$62.57" was displayed on the screen. I punched in a sixty dollar withdrawal, accepted a $2.50 charge for using the machine, and walked back out with the cash. I placed the money in the sobbing woman's hand, while saying nothing.

As she went to speak, I placed my finger onto my lips as if to imply silence, and turned, walking out of the store.

So here I sit on the beach, a lone man, the unlikely minimalist, writing this essay as I finish drinking the last few sips from this wine bottle. I remembered that wondrous moment from long ago, when I received the news from the intensive care unit. The swelling had subsided, and the breathing tube had been removed. My precious child was going to be okay.

I had finally found the truth, the chains of possessions unshackled,
The slavery of obligation abolished; a conscience clear.

I had sought fortune, and found it, only to see it sift through my fingers like the sands on the beach.

Yet through all this, and above all else, I realize that I do indeed possess treasures, treasures and riches beyond any creation of man.

I have life; I have air to breathe, and I have an amazingly abundant planet to live on, and so do my children, and my grandchildren.

And that is all that I need."

Photo courtesy of Karen Wood

Acknowledgements

Hurricane Michael was a pivotal, life changing event for many, each of us learning to cope with our situations in different ways. I found an undiscovered talent for writing, A new-found avenue in which to express myself, as I went on my journey to make sense of it all.

There were obstacles, disguised as fear, doubt, and uncertainty, as if anyone could possibly be interested in what I had to say. I began to post my jottings on social media in order to gain feedback, if any.

It was there that I realized the true power of a kind word, or just a short note from someone who took the time to let me know that it was appreciated, and that I should keep writing. It was the fuel I needed to stay at it, and I appreciate your comments beyond words.

Special Thanks to my Son, Justin Michael, for planting the seed in my mind to write down my experiences after the storm, little did he know that seed would sprout like Jacks beanstalk, and I would harvest the bumper crop of creativity and joy that writing has offered me.

Thank you to Ms. Melodie Denson, a regular guest at the little motel, that offered her editing skills; she kept my redundancy from becoming repetitious, my repetitions from being redundant, and taught me to never talk politics at a book club meeting..

My hats off to Ms. Lacy Gray, for the amazing photograph that to me, embodied the essence of Hurricane Michael better than any other;

Appreciation to Ms. Karen Holland Wood, whom I taught long ago how to take photographs, but she in turn showed me how to make magic with the camera lens;

A solemn thank you from my heart to Ms. Kaye Atchinson. Ms. Kaye was a longtime friend of mine in Mexico Beach, who retired to an assisted living facility in Auburn, Alabama. Ms. Kaye took a great interest in my writing, so much that when I sent her my manuscript, she wrote me a seven page letter explaining how much she enjoyed it, and offered advice on how to navigate through the "writing career" that she felt lay in my future.

Ms.Kaye was a teacher, a librarian, a mentor, and a friend. She and I spoke regularly on messenger, and one night I asked her if she would be interested in writing a Foreword, or introduction to the diary, a task which not only did she readily accept, but accomplished beautifully, and I took the liberty to place it on the back cover of this book.

Sadly, Ms. Kaye never got to see her words in print, as she passed away from complications from surgery before publication, but I pray her kind words and comments will live on through the readers of this book, and remain in my heart forever.

About the Author

Michael Lee Kent is an author, photographer, cartoonist, musician, builder, father, grandfather, and Hurricane Michael survivor. He lives in Mexico Beach, Florida with his four-legged buddy, Jake. This is his first collection of stories.

Made in the USA
Columbia, SC
30 January 2025